The Home Chosen

AMEYA VATSA

Published by AMEYA VATSA, 2024.

Table of Contents

1. The Call of the Unknown 1

2. Preparing Your Mind and Spirit 5

3. The Art of Summoning 9

4. Understanding the UFO Phenomenon 13

5. Experiences of Contact 17

6. Astral Travel and UFO Connection 21

7. Community and Support 25

8. Raising Your Vibrational Frequency 29

9. Nature's Role in UFO Summoning 33

10. Aligning with the Cosmic Energy 37

11. The Role of Sound and Frequency 41

12. Overcoming Fears and Doubts 45

13. Documenting Your Journey 49

14. Lessons from the Stars 53

15. The Future of UFO Summoning and Spirituality 57

For those questioning, "Why am I here?".

Chapter 1: The Soul's Resting Place

The Beginning of Arya's Journey

In the boundless expanse of the celestial realms, a soul floated gently, bathed in the soft glow of an eternal light that had no source, yet was everywhere. The space around her pulsed with peace and stillness, a place where time itself seemed to dissolve into the infinite. Arya had been here many times before—this vast expanse was both familiar and comforting. It was a place where souls rested between lives, preparing for their next journey.

As Arya drifted, she sensed a presence nearby. It was Zafira, a radiant being whose light shimmered like the soft glow of a thousand stars. Zafira's energy was soothing, filled with the quiet wisdom of a spirit who had guided countless souls before Arya. Beside her was Kalan, his energy strong and grounding, like the deep roots of an ancient tree. Together, they had been Arya's guides through many lifetimes.

"Arya," Zafira's voice resonated in the stillness, though it wasn't a voice as one would hear on Earth—it was more like a vibration, a thought that seemed to come from the core of her being.

Arya opened her awareness to her guides, sensing their loving presence.

"Is it time again?" Arya asked, although in this realm, words were not necessary. Her thoughts and emotions flowed directly to her guides, and their responses returned the same way.

Zafira nodded, her essence brightening in confirmation. "It is. You have rested long enough. There is a new journey ahead."

Arya paused. The thought of returning to Earth stirred a mixture of emotions within her—curiosity, excitement, but also apprehension. Earth was a place of dense energy, where lessons could be hard and painful. Here, in the celestial realms, everything was clear, everything made sense. But on Earth, with its veil of forgetfulness, the soul's connection to its higher truth could be easily lost.

"What have I not learned yet?" Arya asked, her energy softly vibrating with concern. "What remains for me on Earth?"

Kalan stepped forward, his presence grounding and steady. "There is much still to be learned," he said gently. "You've chosen this path before, and with each life, you've grown. But there are deeper lessons—lessons of the heart and soul that can only be understood in the material world."

A vision began to unfold before Arya, projected from Kalan's energy. She saw glimpses of her past lives—snapshots of moments where her soul had struggled, triumphed, and grown. There were scenes of joy, but also of suffering—times when she had fallen short of her spiritual goals, where old patterns had repeated and held her back from true understanding.

"You've carried these karmic threads with you across many lives," Zafira explained. "Each time you return, you are given the opportunity to unravel them, to heal what has not yet been healed."

Arya gazed at the vision, feeling the weight of her unresolved karma. Though she had lived many lives, there were still moments where anger, fear, and attachment had clouded her soul's clarity. She understood that Earth was a school—a place where souls went to experience the full spectrum of emotions and learn the lessons they couldn't learn in the higher realms.

"I know," Arya said softly, "but why must it be so hard? Why must we suffer to grow?"

Zafira's light dimmed slightly, a gesture of empathy. "The suffering you experience is not a punishment, Arya. It is simply a reflection of the duality of Earth. In the higher realms, where we are now, everything is light, love, and understanding. But Earth operates on a different set of rules. The soul must navigate through both light and shadow, through love and fear, in order to truly know itself."

Kalan's energy pulsed with strength. "Remember, Arya, that Earth is a place of great potential. It is where souls can accelerate their growth in ways that are not possible here. The density of the physical world, the limitations of the human body, and the emotions that come with being incarnate—these are the very challenges that can bring you closer to understanding your divine nature."

Arya was silent for a moment, absorbing their words. She knew, deep within her being, that they were right. There had been times in her past lives when, through the most difficult trials, she had found the greatest insights. When the soul was pushed to its limits, it could transcend those limits and remember its true nature. But the thought of going back, of facing those trials again, still filled her with hesitation.

"Will I be alone this time?" Arya asked, her thoughts echoing her deepest fear. "Will I remember who I truly am, or will I get lost again?"

Zafira moved closer, her light surrounding Arya in a comforting embrace. "You will never be alone. We will be with you, even if you cannot see or hear us in the same way. And you will not go without guidance. Before you are born, you will create a soul contract—an agreement that will help guide you through your life. It will include the lessons you need to learn, the people you will meet, and the challenges you will face."

Kalan added, "And though you may forget the details of this plan when you are on Earth, there will always be signs—small reminders from your higher self and the universe that will help you stay on your path. Intuition, synchronicities, the people you are drawn to—these will all be your guides."

Arya felt a flicker of hope. She had been through this process many times, yet the reassurance that she would be guided through the next journey gave her some comfort.

"I trust you," Arya said at last. "But I need to understand more before I make my decision."

"Of course," Zafira said softly. "There is much to discuss before you commit to this new life. Let us take you to the Cosmic Council. They will help you see the full picture."

The Journey to the Council

Zafira and Kalan gently led Arya through the celestial realms. Here, space was not defined by distance, but by energy. They moved swiftly, gliding through currents of light and sound that wove together in a harmonious dance. Arya felt herself expanding, becoming more aware of the interconnectedness of all souls, the intricate web of energy that united them.

In the distance, a magnificent structure came into view—a vast hall made entirely of light, shimmering with a thousand hues that shifted and flowed like water. This was the Cosmic Council, the place where souls gathered to review their past lives and plan their future incarnations.

As they approached, Arya felt a sense of awe wash over her. The Council was not made up of individuals, but of a collective consciousness—a group of ancient souls who had transcended the need for individual identity. They existed in pure unity, embodying the wisdom of countless lifetimes.

"Arya," the voice of the Council resonated within her, surrounding her with a warmth and familiarity that eased her fears. "You have come seeking guidance for your next life."

"Yes," Arya replied, her energy steady but curious. "I want to understand why I must return to Earth. What is it that I still need to learn?"

The light around her swirled, and in an instant, Arya found herself surrounded by visions. These were not just glimpses of her past lives—they were moments of deep significance, each one carrying the weight of a lesson unfinished.

She saw herself as a child in one life, filled with anger and resentment toward those who had wronged her. In another, she was an old woman, filled with regret for not having forgiven those who had hurt her. In yet another life, she saw herself caught in a cycle of attachment, unable to let go of material possessions and relationships that no longer served her.

"You have carried these patterns with you," the Council said, "across many lifetimes. Each time, you have been given the opportunity to heal them, and while you have made progress, there is still more to be done."

Arya watched the scenes unfold, feeling the emotions tied to each one. She had been so close, so many times, to breaking free from these patterns. But each time, something had held her back—fear, anger, attachment. She realized now that these were the very lessons she needed to master in her next life.

"I see now," Arya said, her energy softening. "But how will I ensure that I don't repeat these mistakes again?"

Understanding the Patterns of Karma

As Arya absorbed the scenes of her past lives, the weight of her choices settled deeply within her essence. These were not isolated incidents, but interconnected threads woven into the fabric of her soul's evolution. The lives she had lived were bound together by karmic patterns—lessons she had come close to mastering, but not yet fully understood. The images, though stark, held a strange beauty, each one a reminder of her journey across time.

"I've seen these moments before," Arya said quietly, her thoughts directed toward the Council. "I know the choices I made and the consequences that followed. But why do these same lessons repeat? How can I break free?"

The light of the Council shifted slightly, as if considering her question. "Karma is not punishment, Arya," they explained, their voice resonating with infinite patience. "It is balance. The choices you make in one life echo into the next, not to trap you, but to offer you the opportunity for deeper understanding. Each lifetime brings you closer to the truth of who you are."

Arya contemplated their words. She had often thought of karma as a kind of debt, something to be repaid. But now, as the Council spoke, she began to see it differently. Karma was not a weight dragging her down—it was the tool she could use to rise.

"So these patterns are not failures," Arya said, more to herself than to the Council. "They're opportunities. If I face them again, I can finally transcend them."

"Exactly," Zafira's voice entered her awareness, soft but firm. "The lessons will continue to present themselves until you learn them completely. And once you do, you are free from their influence."

Arya's thoughts swirled with possibilities. She was beginning to understand that her repeated struggles—her unresolved anger, her attachments, her fear of loss—were not curses, but gifts. Each one was an invitation to grow, to reach new levels of compassion, forgiveness, and understanding.

"But how do I ensure that I learn this time?" Arya asked, turning to her guides. "What if I get lost in the human experience again? It's so easy to forget the truth when you're on Earth, surrounded by all the distractions."

Zafira's light pulsed with warmth. "That is where your soul contract will guide you. Before you are born, you will make certain agreements—not only with yourself but with others. These agreements will help steer you toward the lessons you need to learn. The people you meet, the relationships you form, the challenges you face—all of these are part of the contract."

Kalan's steady presence added weight to Zafira's words. "And you will not be alone. Even in the moments when you feel lost, your higher self will always be there, sending you signs and synchronicities. You will feel the pull toward certain paths, and if you listen to your intuition, it will guide you."

Arya nodded slowly, the enormity of what they were saying sinking in. She had lived many lives before, but this time felt different. There was a clarity here that she hadn't experienced before—a sense that this next life could be the one where she finally understood.

"I am ready," Arya said, her voice stronger now. "I want to create my soul contract."

The Council's light swirled again, this time shifting to a soft golden hue. "Before you create your contract, there is one more thing you must understand, Arya. The choices you make in this contract will determine the trajectory of your next life. You must choose with care."

The Power of Choice

The scene around Arya changed once more. She now found herself in a vast open space, where threads of light crisscrossed in every direction, weaving an intricate web of possibilities. Each thread represented a different choice, a different path she could take in her upcoming life. Some threads were bright and clear, others darker and more difficult, but all were connected.

"This is the web of possibilities," Kalan explained. "Each soul has the power to choose the path they will walk. Some choices will lead to growth and healing, while others may lead to repetition and stagnation. But all choices are valuable, for they bring new experiences."

Arya reached out, tentatively touching one of the glowing threads. As she did, a vision unfolded before her—a future life filled with love and harmony, where she would be surrounded by supportive relationships and peaceful circumstances. The life seemed easy, almost too easy. She felt a deep sense of contentment in the vision, but something was missing. The growth, the challenge—it wasn't there.

She released the thread and reached for another. This one was darker, its light dimmed by shadows. As she touched it, a new vision appeared. In this life, she would face great hardships—loss, betrayal, illness. The emotions were intense, overwhelming even. But beneath the surface, Arya could sense something else—a deep undercurrent of strength and resilience. This life would be hard, but it would offer the greatest opportunity for her soul to grow.

Arya withdrew her hand, contemplating the choices before her.

"You see now why the choice is so important," Zafira said softly. "You can choose a life of ease, where you will find joy and comfort, but the opportunities for growth will be limited. Or you can choose a path that challenges you, where the lessons will be difficult, but the rewards will be great."

Arya was silent, feeling the weight of the decision before her. She had lived both kinds of lives before—those filled with comfort and those filled with struggle. But this time, she wanted something different. She wanted to face the lessons she had avoided in the past, to finally break free from the patterns that had held her back.

"I choose the harder path," Arya said at last, her voice steady. "I want to grow, even if it means facing pain and hardship."

Kalan's light brightened in approval. "A wise choice, Arya. The hardest paths often lead to the greatest growth."

Zafira stepped forward, her energy surrounding Arya in a comforting embrace. "Now we will help you create your soul contract."

The Soul Contract Begins

Arya sat with her guides, the web of possibilities still shimmering around her. Together, they began to craft her soul contract, carefully selecting the experiences that would help her learn the lessons she needed.

"You will choose your family," Zafira said, her voice gentle but firm. "The people you are born to will shape your early life. They will either support you or challenge you, but they will play a crucial role in your growth."

Arya felt a tug in her consciousness as a vision of a family appeared before her. The mother, strong and loving, would teach her the importance of compassion and selflessness. The father, distant and cold, would challenge her to find love within herself, rather than seeking it externally. She saw siblings, each with their own roles to play—one a guide, the other a rival.

"I choose them," Arya said, feeling a sense of recognition as she gazed at the vision of her future family. "I know these souls. We've been together before."

Zafira nodded. "You will find that many of the souls you meet in your life will be familiar. You have traveled together through many lifetimes, helping each other to grow."

Kalan continued, "Now you must choose your challenges. These will be the moments in your life that test you, that push you to grow beyond your current limitations."

Arya reached out, touching several threads. With each one, a different challenge appeared before her—illness, heartbreak, loss. The emotions tied to each one were intense, but Arya knew they were necessary.

"I choose these," she said, her voice firm. "I want to face these challenges so that I can finally learn to let go of my attachments and find peace within myself."

Zafira's light shimmered with approval. "You are brave, Arya. These choices will help you grow in ways you cannot yet imagine."

Kalan's energy was steady and grounding. "Now that your contract is almost complete, there is one final choice you must make. You must choose the purpose of your life—the lesson that will guide you through all the others. What is the one thing you want to learn in this lifetime?"

Arya thought deeply, searching her soul for the answer. After a moment, she spoke, her voice filled with clarity. "I want to learn how to love unconditionally. I've struggled with it in my past lives—holding onto anger, resentment, and fear. But this time, I want to learn how to love without conditions, without attachment. I want to love freely, no matter what happens."

Zafira's light brightened, filling the space with warmth. "A noble choice, Arya. Love is the highest lesson a soul can learn."

The contract was complete. Arya felt a deep sense of peace as she gazed at the web of possibilities before her. She had made her choices with care, guided by her soul's desire for growth and healing.

"Are you ready?" Zafira asked, her voice gentle.

Arya took a deep breath, her energy steady. "I am ready."

With that, the scene around her began to shift once more, preparing her for the next stage of her journey—the moment when she would step through the veil and begin her new life on Earth.

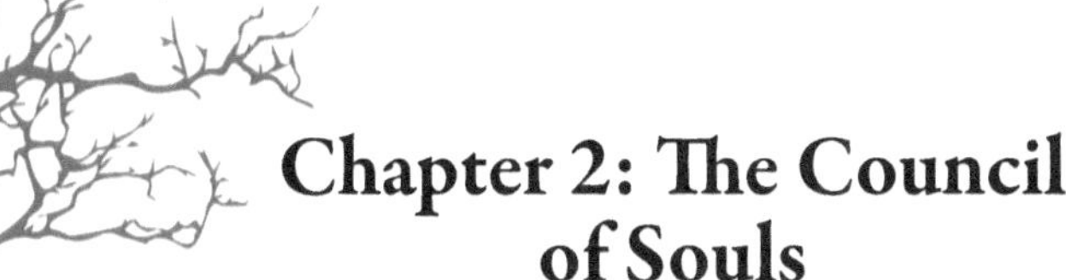

Chapter 2: The Council of Souls

A Meeting with the Council

As Arya prepared herself for what lay ahead, the radiant light of the Cosmic Council intensified, shimmering in hues of gold and silver. She could feel the power and wisdom emanating from the collective consciousness of the ancient souls who made up the Council. Though they were not individuals in the human sense, each one carried the essence of countless lifetimes and the deep understanding that came with such experience.

"Welcome, Arya," the voice of the Council echoed softly, resonating not just in her mind, but in the very core of her being. "You have chosen to return to Earth, and we are here to help you understand the lessons that await you."

The presence of Zafira and Kalan stood firm at Arya's side, their energies guiding her gently as she stepped forward into the sacred space of the Council. Around her, swirling visions began to form, each one a glimpse into the lives she had lived before.

Arya found herself drawn into one particular vision—a life where she had been a young woman, filled with ambition and fire. In that life, she had sought power and success, driven by a deep need to prove herself to the world. But along the way, she had hurt others, letting her ego and pride cloud her judgment. She had climbed high, but the price had been the relationships she had sacrificed—her family, her friends, and even her own sense of peace.

"You have lived many lives like this one," the Council said, their tone gentle yet firm. "Each time, you have sought to control your external circumstances, believing that power, wealth, and status would bring you fulfillment. But what did you learn, Arya?"

Arya felt the weight of the question. The memories from that life came flooding back—the achievements, the accolades, and the loneliness that followed. She had reached the top, but it had left her empty.

"I learned that true fulfillment doesn't come from external success," Arya said quietly. "I had everything I thought I wanted, but I still felt lost. I hurt people along the way, and in the end, I hurt myself. I learned that love and connection are more important than anything material."

The Council's light pulsed softly as if nodding in agreement. "Yes. That was an important lesson, but it is one you have struggled with across many lives. The need for control, for external validation, has been a recurring theme for you. In your next life, you will face similar challenges. You will be tested, and you will have the opportunity to choose love over power, connection over control."

Arya absorbed the words, understanding that these patterns had followed her through lifetimes. Each life had offered her a chance to learn, but in many, she had fallen into the same traps—seeking validation outside herself, chasing success at the expense of her soul's true desires.

"But how do I break free from this pattern?" Arya asked, her voice filled with a quiet urgency. "How do I ensure that I don't repeat the same mistakes again?"

Zafira stepped forward, her energy calm and reassuring. "The key is awareness, Arya. In your next life, you will be given moments of choice—moments where you will feel the pull of your old patterns. But if you can remain aware, if you can pause and listen to your heart, you will have the power to choose a different path. Each time you choose love over fear, connection over separation, you will rewrite the script of your karma."

Kalan's deep voice resonated beside her. "And remember, Arya, that even when you fall, even when you stumble and repeat old patterns, it is not a failure. Each life offers multiple opportunities to grow. You will not be judged for your mistakes, but you will be asked to learn from them. That is the purpose of karma—not to punish, but to teach."

Arya nodded, feeling the truth of their words. She had known the pain of her own choices in past lives, but she had also known moments of deep connection, moments when she had chosen love and compassion over ego and fear. It was those moments she wanted to cultivate in her next life.

The Choice of Souls

As the vision of Arya's past life faded, another took its place. This time, she saw herself as a mother in a small village, living a simple life. She had cared deeply for her family, pouring her love and energy into raising her children. In that life, she had known joy, but also great sorrow. She had lost one of her children to illness, and the grief had nearly broken her.

"You have known great love, but also great loss," the Council said. "In this life, you learned the power of unconditional love. But you also learned the pain of attachment—the fear of losing those you love."

Arya remembered that life well. She had loved her children fiercely, but when her son had died, she had been unable to accept it. She had clung to the pain, letting it consume her. In her grief, she had turned away from her other children, unable to move past the loss.

"You learned an important lesson in that life," Zafira said softly. "Love is not about possession. You cannot hold on to those you love, for they are not yours to keep. In your next life, you will be asked to love without attachment, to love freely, even in the face of loss."

Arya felt the familiar ache in her heart, the lingering sorrow from that life. She had loved so deeply, but she had also suffered because of that love. Could she really learn to love without fear? Without the need to hold on?

"You are stronger than you know," Kalan said, his voice grounding her. "Each life has prepared you for the next. You have learned love, and you have learned loss. Now you must learn to hold both in balance—to love fully, but without attachment, without fear. That is one of the great lessons of Earth."

Arya understood now that her next life would not be without pain. She would love, and she would lose. But this time, she would have the opportunity to face that loss with grace, to find peace in the knowledge that love transcends the physical world.

"I'm ready to learn," Arya said, her voice steady. "I want to love without fear. I want to find peace, even in loss."

The Council's light shimmered brightly, and Arya felt their approval wash over her. "You have made a wise choice, Arya. These lessons will not be easy, but they will bring you great growth."

A Deeper Understanding of Karma

As the visions faded once more, Arya found herself standing before the Council, feeling a sense of clarity and purpose. She now understood the deeper lessons she would face in her next life—the need to let go of control, the importance of love without attachment, and the challenge of breaking free from old karmic patterns.

But there was still one question that weighed on her mind.

"What about the people in my life?" Arya asked, turning to Zafira. "I know that I will face my own challenges, but what about those who will be with me? The souls I will meet on Earth—how do they fit into this?"

Zafira smiled softly, her light radiating warmth. "The people you meet in your life are not random, Arya. Many of them are souls you have traveled with across lifetimes. Together, you have agreed to help each other grow, to play certain roles in each other's lives. Some will be your guides, others will challenge you, and still others will reflect back to you the lessons you need to learn."

Kalan stepped forward, his energy grounding Arya once more. "These souls will come into your life at exactly the right time. Some will stay with you for your entire life, while others may only appear briefly. But each one will serve a purpose."

Arya thought about the people she had known in her past lives—the friends who had supported her, the lovers who had taught her about vulnerability, and even the enemies who had pushed her to grow in ways she hadn't expected. In each life, there had been relationships that shaped her journey, for better or for worse.

"So we choose these relationships before we are born?" Arya asked, her curiosity piqued.

"Yes," Zafira said. "Before you incarnate, you will meet with the souls who will play important roles in your life. Together, you will create agreements—soul contracts—that outline the lessons you will help each other learn. These contracts are not set in stone, but they serve as a guide, a blueprint for your life."

Arya nodded slowly, beginning to grasp the complexity of the web of relationships that would form in her next life. She understood now that every encounter, every relationship, was an opportunity for growth—whether it brought joy or pain.

"But what about free will?" Arya asked, her thoughts drifting to the concept of destiny versus choice. "If we make these contracts before we're born, does that mean everything is predetermined? Do we have any control over what happens?"

Kalan's light brightened as he answered. "Free will and destiny exist together, Arya. The soul contracts you create are like a map, but you are always free to choose how you navigate that map. You may choose to follow the path laid out for you, or you may choose to go in a different direction. Both are valuable. Even when you stray from the path, you are still learning. The choices you make on Earth shape your destiny, but they do not bind you to it."

Arya felt a sense of relief wash over her. The idea that she could make choices, that she had control over her own fate, was comforting. She understood now that while the soul contracts provided a framework, it was up to her to decide how she would live her life.

"I see," Arya said quietly. "We have a plan, but we also have the freedom to change that plan."

"Exactly," Zafira said, her light softening in approval. "And even when you make choices that take you off the path, your higher self will always guide you back, offering you opportunities to realign with your soul's purpose."

Preparing for the Journey

The Council's light began to shift, signaling the end of their meeting. Arya felt a deep sense of peace as the weight of her past lives, her karma, and her future choices settled into place. She was ready to begin the next phase of her journey—ready to create her soul contract and step into her new life on Earth.

But before she could leave, there was one final message from the Council.

"Remember, Arya," their voice echoed softly, "you are never alone. You are part of a greater whole, connected to all souls across time and space. In your darkest moments, when you feel lost or afraid, remember this: You are loved, and you are guided. Always."

With those words, the light of the Council began to fade, and Arya felt herself being gently pulled back toward the celestial realm where Zafira and Kalan waited for her.

As they moved through the infinite space, Arya felt a sense of purpose and clarity growing within her. She knew that the path ahead would not be easy, but she also knew that she had the strength and wisdom to navigate it. With Zafira and Kalan by her side, she was ready to take the next step.

"Let's create your soul contract," Zafira said, her voice filled with gentle encouragement. "It's time to prepare for your life on Earth."

Arya nodded, her energy steady and resolute. She was ready. Ready to face the challenges, the lessons, and the opportunities that awaited her. Ready to embrace love without fear, to let go of control, and to find peace in the knowledge that every choice she made would bring her closer to the truth of her soul.

With a deep breath, Arya stepped forward, ready to begin the process of creating the blueprint for her next life—the life that would help her grow, heal, and evolve.

Chapter 3: Karma and the Law of Cause and Effect

Unraveling the Threads of Karma

Arya stood in a vast expanse of light, surrounded by the comforting presence of Zafira and Kalan. Their luminous forms shimmered softly as they prepared her for the next phase of her journey. Having just left the Cosmic Council, where her past lives were laid bare, Arya now understood more deeply the patterns she had carried through her many incarnations. But there was still much to grasp—especially when it came to the complex web of karma.

"Karma is like a river," Zafira said, her voice filled with a quiet grace. "It flows through each of your lives, carrying with it the energy of every choice you've made. Some choices create smooth waters, while others create turbulence. But every ripple in the river has a purpose. It teaches you something about yourself."

Arya listened intently, her mind absorbing the metaphor. She had heard about karma in her previous incarnations, but now, here in this place of pure understanding, it took on new meaning. Karma wasn't about punishment or reward—it was about balance, about the energy one created and how it returned to them in various forms.

"You've been entangled in certain karmic patterns," Kalan continued, his voice grounding her in its steady presence. "These patterns are not mistakes—they are opportunities. Each time you face them, you get closer to breaking free. It's not about avoiding karma, but about transforming it."

The air around Arya shimmered as a vision began to unfold before her once again. This time, it wasn't a specific past life, but a series of events, connected by an invisible thread. In one life, she had abandoned someone in need, prioritizing her own desires over their well-being. In another, she had been the one abandoned, left to struggle without support. The energy of her choices, both in giving and receiving, wove together into a complex tapestry, a karmic cycle of cause and effect.

"I see it now," Arya said softly. "Each action creates a ripple that comes back to me in different forms. When I hurt others, that energy eventually returns, not as punishment, but as a way for me to understand the impact of my choices."

"Exactly," Zafira said with warmth in her voice. "You are not being punished for your mistakes, Arya. You are being given the chance to experience both sides of the coin, so that you can understand the full spectrum of love, fear, kindness, and cruelty. This is how souls evolve."

The vision shifted, showing Arya a moment from one of her earlier lives. She had been a man of power, wealthy and influential, but her decisions had often come at the expense of others. She had prioritized her own needs, blind to the suffering around her. Now, in her current spiritual state, she could see the effect of those choices—how the energy of selfishness had returned to her in later lives, in the form of isolation, loneliness, and loss.

"You've experienced both sides now," Kalan said, his energy strong but kind. "You've lived lives of abundance, and you've lived lives of lack. You've been the one with power, and you've been the one oppressed by power. The balance is beginning to form, and your next life will give you the opportunity to break free from these cycles."

Arya felt a sense of clarity wash over her. She had often wondered why certain lives had been filled with hardship, why certain relationships had seemed doomed from the start. Now she understood—these were not random experiences. They were echoes of her own choices, giving her the chance to grow and to heal the wounds she had both inflicted and endured.

"I want to release these patterns," Arya said, her voice filled with determination. "I don't want to carry this karma with me any longer."

Zafira's light brightened, her energy filled with approval. "And you can, Arya. But releasing karma isn't about avoiding challenges—it's about embracing them. It's about meeting your experiences with love, even when they are difficult. It's about making choices that are aligned with your higher self, rather than repeating old patterns out of fear or habit."

Arya nodded, feeling the weight of Zafira's words. She knew this wouldn't be easy. Her past lives had shown her how deeply ingrained these patterns were—how easy it was to fall into the same traps of fear, anger, and attachment. But she also knew that with awareness, she could choose differently.

Choosing to Transform Karma

As Arya stood before the web of her past choices, she felt a deep sense of responsibility. The choices she had made in previous lives had created the circumstances she faced in each incarnation, but now she had the opportunity to change. With her soul contract still to be written, she knew that the life she was about to enter would be pivotal. It was her chance to transform the karma she had carried for so long.

"You have already done much of the work," Kalan said, his voice steady and reassuring. "Your awareness of these patterns is the first step toward breaking them. In your next life, you will face moments where you are tempted to fall back into old habits. But with each choice, you can create a new path."

Zafira stepped forward, her energy warm and supportive. "When you feel the pull of your old karma, remember this: You are not bound by your past. You have the power to choose differently. Each moment is a chance to align with your higher self, to choose love over fear, to choose compassion over anger. This is how karma is transformed."

Arya felt a sense of hope rising within her. She had always thought of karma as something that controlled her, something she couldn't escape. But now she saw it as an opportunity—a chance to learn, to grow, and to become the person her soul was meant to be.

"How do I choose differently?" Arya asked, her voice filled with curiosity. "What do I need to do to break these patterns?"

"Awareness is the key," Kalan said. "When you are aware of the patterns you carry, you can see them as they arise in your life. The temptation to react out of fear, anger, or attachment will always be there, but if you can pause, reflect, and choose a different response, you will begin to rewrite your karma."

Zafira's light shimmered softly. "It's not about perfection, Arya. It's about intention. Each time you choose love, each time you choose to act with kindness and compassion, you are shifting the energy of your karma. And with each shift, you move closer to true freedom."

Arya absorbed their words, feeling a deep sense of purpose. She knew that her next life would be filled with challenges, but now she felt prepared. She understood that each challenge was an opportunity to grow, to learn, and to break free from the cycles that had held her back for so long.

The Ripple Effect of Choice

As Arya continued to reflect on her karmic journey, another vision unfolded before her. This time, she saw a moment from one of her most recent lives—a life where she had made a small but profound choice. In that life, she had been a young woman struggling with resentment toward a family member. For years, she had harbored anger and bitterness, believing that this person had wronged her. But in one pivotal moment, she had chosen to forgive.

The vision showed her the ripple effect of that choice. By letting go of her anger, she had not only healed herself, but had also shifted the energy between herself and her family member. Their relationship had transformed from one of tension and conflict to one of understanding and love. And that energy had continued to ripple outward, affecting the lives of those around them in ways Arya hadn't even realized.

"Every choice you make affects not only your own karma, but the karma of those around you," Zafira explained. "When you choose love, you send that energy out into the world, and it creates ripples that can transform lives. This is the power of karma—it is not just about your own growth, but about the growth of all souls."

Arya watched the vision, feeling the profound impact of that single choice. It had seemed small at the time—just a moment of forgiveness—but now she saw how that one decision had created a wave of healing that extended far beyond herself.

"I had no idea," Arya said softly. "I didn't realize how much my choices affected others."

Kalan's voice was filled with gentle wisdom. "That is the beauty of karma, Arya. It connects all souls in a web of energy, where every action, every thought, every choice has an impact. When you choose love, you elevate not only yourself, but those around you. And when others do the same, it creates a collective shift toward healing and growth."

Arya felt a sense of awe as she considered the vastness of karma. It was not just about her own journey, but about the journey of all souls. Every choice she made was part of a larger tapestry, woven together by the actions and intentions of countless beings across time and space.

Preparing to Break the Cycle

With this new understanding of karma, Arya felt a renewed sense of purpose. She knew that her next life would be her opportunity to break free from the cycles that had bound her for so long. But more than that, she knew that her choices could help heal not only her own soul, but the souls of those she encountered on Earth.

"You have chosen a challenging path," Zafira said, her light warm and reassuring. "But it is one that will bring you great growth. You have the opportunity to transform your karma in this life, to break free from the patterns that have held you back, and to help others do the same."

Kalan's energy was steady and grounding. "Remember, Arya, that you are never alone in this journey. The people you meet in your next life—the souls who will cross your path—are all part of the same web. Some will challenge you, some will support you, but all will offer you opportunities to grow."

Arya nodded, feeling the weight of their words. She knew that her next life would not be easy, but she also knew that it would be filled with moments of choice—moments where she could choose to act from a place of love, compassion, and awareness. And in doing so, she would not only heal herself but contribute to the healing of the world around her.

"I'm ready," Arya said, her voice filled with quiet determination. "I'm ready to face whatever challenges come my way, and I'm ready to choose differently this time."

Zafira and Kalan stood by her side, their energies radiating love and support.

"And we will be with you every step of the way," Zafira said softly. "You are never truly alone, Arya. Even when the path seems difficult, remember that we are here, guiding you, helping you navigate the currents of karma. And most importantly, remember that you have the power to transform your life, one choice at a time."

Arya felt a sense of peace settle over her. She was ready for the next chapter of her journey, ready to write her soul contract and step into the life that awaited her on Earth. With her heart full of purpose and her mind clear, she knew that this life would be the one where she finally broke free from the cycles of karma and found the freedom her soul had been seeking.

Chapter 4: Free Will and Soul Contracts

The Power of Free Will

Arya stood in the vast expanse of light, contemplating the enormity of the choices that lay before her. In the higher realms, where everything was illuminated by the clarity of the soul's purpose, the idea of free will was understood in its purest form. But Arya knew that once she incarnated on Earth, that clarity would fade, and the freedom of choice would become more complex, entangled with emotions, desires, and the struggles of the human experience.

"You have the power to choose," Zafira's voice echoed gently in her consciousness. "The path of your next life is not predetermined, Arya. The soul contract you are about to create is a guide, but it is not a rigid script. At every moment, you have the freedom to choose which direction to take, how to respond to the challenges and opportunities you will face."

Arya took a deep breath, feeling the weight of her choices settling within her. "But what about destiny?" she asked, her thoughts drifting to the idea that some things in life were meant to happen. "Isn't there a part of my life that is already set? The people I will meet, the lessons I must learn?"

Kalan's light brightened beside her, his presence grounding and steady. "Yes, there are certain events, relationships, and circumstances that are woven into your soul contract before you are born. These are the experiences you have chosen to help you grow. But how you respond to them, how you navigate those experiences—that is entirely up to you. Free will and destiny are not opposites, Arya. They work together, giving you both structure and freedom."

A vision began to form in the air before Arya. She saw a long, winding path, illuminated by the soft glow of starlight. Along the path were markers—points of significance that stood out from the rest of the journey. Some were bright and glowing, representing moments of joy, love, and connection. Others were dimmer, surrounded by shadows, representing challenges and pain. But the path between the markers was fluid, shifting and changing with each step she took.

"This is your life," Zafira explained. "The markers are your destiny—the significant moments you have chosen before incarnating, the key events that will help you fulfill your soul's purpose. But the path between them is where free will comes in. How you move from one marker to the next, the choices you make along the way—that is where your power lies."

Arya watched the path unfold, understanding now that her life would be a dance between fate and choice. She would encounter certain people and situations, but the way she responded, the lessons she chose to learn or resist, would shape the course of her journey.

"But what if I make the wrong choices?" Arya asked, her voice filled with concern. "What if I stray too far from my purpose?"

Zafira's light pulsed gently with reassurance. "There are no wrong choices, Arya. Every choice you make brings with it a lesson. Even when you stray from the path, you are still learning. And the universe will always offer you opportunities to realign with your soul's purpose. There will be signs, synchronicities, and moments of clarity that will help guide you back."

Kalan added, "And remember, Arya, that the goal is not perfection. The purpose of life on Earth is to learn, and learning often involves making mistakes, experiencing setbacks, and growing through challenges. What matters is not that you avoid making the wrong choices, but that you remain open to learning from each experience."

Arya felt a wave of relief wash over her. The idea that there were no wrong choices, only opportunities for growth, lifted a weight from her heart. She understood now that life was not a test she had to pass, but a journey of exploration, where each step was a chance to learn more about herself and her soul's purpose.

Crafting the Soul Contract

With this newfound understanding, Arya felt ready to begin crafting her soul contract. She knew that the contract would be a map for her life on Earth, outlining the key experiences she would encounter, the relationships that would shape her, and the lessons she had chosen to learn. But she also understood that the contract was not rigid. It was a flexible blueprint, a guide that would help her navigate her journey, but one that allowed for the freedom of choice at every turn.

Zafira and Kalan stood by her side as she began to weave the threads of her next life. Arya could feel the energy of her intentions taking shape, forming the outline of her contract.

"First, you must choose your life's overarching purpose," Zafira said, her voice filled with quiet wisdom. "This is the central theme of your life, the guiding lesson that will shape your experiences. Everything else in your contract will be built around this purpose."

Arya closed her eyes and searched within herself. She thought about the lessons she had learned in her past lives, the patterns of karma she was ready to release, and the deeper truths she wanted to embody in her next incarnation. She knew that love was at the heart of everything—love without attachment, love without fear. That was the lesson she had struggled with across many lifetimes, and now she was ready to embrace it fully.

"I want to learn how to love unconditionally," Arya said, her voice steady. "I want to love freely, without attachment or fear. I want to understand that love is not about possession, but about connection and compassion."

Zafira's light brightened in approval. "A noble purpose, Arya. Love is the highest lesson a soul can learn, and it will guide you through every experience you encounter in your next life."

As Arya made this choice, she felt the energy of her soul contract begin to solidify. The intention to love unconditionally became the foundation upon which the rest of her life would be built. But there were still many decisions to make, and Arya knew that each choice would shape the details of her journey.

Choosing Life's Relationships

With her life's purpose in place, Arya now turned her attention to the relationships she would encounter on Earth. She knew that the people she met would play a crucial role in her growth, and that many of them were souls she had traveled with through countless lifetimes.

"You will meet many souls in your next life," Kalan said, his energy grounding her. "Some will be your greatest teachers, others will challenge you in ways you cannot yet imagine. But each one will offer you the opportunity to grow and to fulfill your soul's purpose."

Arya watched as the energy of her soul contract shifted, and visions of different souls began to appear before her. She saw her future family, friends, and lovers—each one connected to her through the intricate web of karma and soul contracts that spanned lifetimes.

"These are the souls you will meet on Earth," Zafira said, her voice soft and reassuring. "Some of them are souls you have known for many lives, while others are new to your journey. But each one has agreed to play a role in your life, to help you learn the lessons you have chosen."

Arya gazed at the vision of her future family. She saw her mother—a strong, compassionate woman who would teach her about the power of unconditional love. She saw her father—a distant, reserved man who would challenge her to find love within herself, rather than seeking it externally. She saw siblings, friends, and romantic partners, each one carrying a unique energy, each one destined to shape her journey in profound ways.

"Do I choose them, or have we already made these agreements?" Arya asked, her voice filled with curiosity.

"These agreements were made long before this moment," Zafira explained. "But now you are choosing to reaffirm them. Each soul has agreed to play a role in your life, just as you have agreed to play a role in theirs. Together, you will help each other grow and evolve."

Arya felt a deep sense of connection as she looked at the souls who would cross her path in her next life. Some of them felt familiar, as though she had known them for lifetimes. Others were new, their energy fresh and unexplored. But she understood now that every relationship, whether easy or challenging, would offer her the opportunity to learn and grow.

Selecting Life's Challenges

With her relationships in place, Arya turned her attention to the challenges she would face on Earth. She knew that life's difficulties were not obstacles, but opportunities for growth. The pain, loss, and hardship she had experienced in previous incarnations had been some of her greatest teachers, and now she was ready to face new challenges with a heart full of courage and determination.

"You will encounter many challenges in your next life," Kalan said, his voice steady and calm. "Some will be physical, others emotional or spiritual. But each one has been chosen by you, to help you learn the lessons you have set for yourself."

Arya reached out and touched the threads of her soul contract, feeling the energy of her future life begin to take shape. She saw visions of illness, heartbreak, and loss—moments of pain that would push her to her limits, but also moments of profound growth and healing.

"I choose these challenges," Arya said, her voice filled with quiet strength. "I know they will be difficult, but I also know they will help me grow. I want to learn how to love even in the face of pain. I want to find peace even in the midst of loss."

Zafira's light shimmered with approval. "You are brave, Arya. These challenges will not break you—they will help you become the person your soul is meant to be."

Arya felt a sense of resolve settle over her. She had faced challenges in her past lives, but this time, she was ready to face them with a new perspective. She knew that each hardship was an opportunity to grow, to deepen her understanding of love, and to fulfill her soul's purpose.

Setting the Stage for Free Will

As Arya crafted the final details of her soul contract, she felt the energy of free will weaving through every choice she made. She understood now that while the contract provided a framework for her life, it was her choices that would ultimately shape her journey. The relationships, challenges, and experiences she had chosen were not fixed—they were opportunities, and it was up to her to decide how she would respond to them.

"You have created a beautiful life, Arya," Zafira said, her voice filled with warmth. "It will be a life of love, growth, and transformation. But remember, nothing is set in stone. Every moment is a chance to choose—to align with your higher self, to act with love and compassion, and to grow in ways you cannot yet imagine."

Kalan's energy was steady beside her. "And even when you face difficult choices, remember that you are not alone. You will have guides, signs, and your own intuition to help you navigate your path. Free will is your greatest gift, Arya. Use it wisely."

Arya felt a deep sense of gratitude as she looked at the life she had crafted. She knew that her journey on Earth would be filled with both joy and sorrow, love and loss. But she also knew that with each choice she made, she had the power to transform her life, to break free from the cycles of karma, and to fulfill her soul's purpose.

"I am ready," Arya said, her voice filled with quiet determination. "I am ready to begin my journey on Earth."

Final Words from the Guides

As Arya stood before her completed soul contract, Zafira and Kalan moved closer, their energies filled with love and support. The contract shimmered before her, a radiant web of light that outlined the key moments of her next life.

"You have done well, Arya," Zafira said softly. "This life will bring you the growth you seek, but it will also bring you love, connection, and joy. Remember that every challenge is an opportunity, and every choice is a chance to align with your higher self."

Kalan's voice was filled with strength. "And remember, Arya, that we will be with you always. Even when you cannot see or hear us, we will be there, guiding you, helping you navigate the currents of life. You are never alone."

Arya felt a wave of emotion rise within her. She knew that once she was born on Earth, the veil of forgetfulness would descend, and the clarity she had now would fade. But she also knew that her guides would be with her, helping her remember the truth of who she was and the purpose she had chosen.

"Thank you," Arya said, her voice filled with gratitude. "I will remember. Even when it's hard, I will try to remember."

Zafira's light shimmered warmly. "You will. And when you forget, we will remind you."

Stepping into the New Life

With her soul contract complete and her heart full of purpose, Arya prepared to take the next step on her journey. The energy around her began to shift, signaling the transition from the celestial realms to the physical world. She could feel the pull of Earth, the dense vibrations of the material plane drawing her closer.

As she stood on the threshold of her new life, Arya took one last moment to reflect on the choices she had made. She knew that the road ahead would be filled with challenges, but she also knew that she had the strength, the wisdom, and the love to navigate it.

"I am ready," Arya said, her voice steady and clear. "I am ready to be born."

With those final words, the light around her began to fade, and Arya felt herself being gently pulled toward the Earth. The veil of forgetfulness began to descend, but deep within her soul, she carried the memory of her purpose, the love of her guides, and the knowledge that she had the power to create her own destiny.

As she crossed the threshold into her new life, Arya felt a quiet sense of peace. She was ready. Ready to face the challenges, to learn the lessons, and to fulfill the promise she had made to herself.

And so, Arya's journey on Earth began.

Chapter 5: The Role of Suffering in Spiritual Growth

The Purpose Behind Pain

Arya stood at the edge of the ethereal plane, her consciousness still adjusting to the weight of the soul contract she had just completed. She had chosen a life filled with both love and challenges, with lessons that would test the depth of her soul's understanding. But one question still lingered in her mind—the question of suffering. In her past lives, Arya had known pain intimately, from the loss of loved ones to the physical and emotional struggles that had shaped her journey on Earth. Yet, in this moment, the clarity of the celestial realms offered her a chance to finally understand why suffering was so necessary.

Zafira, always radiant in her presence, moved closer to Arya, sensing the question that stirred in her heart. "You are wondering why suffering must exist," Zafira said softly, her voice gentle as a breeze.

Arya turned to her guide, her thoughts filled with the weight of her past lives. "I understand that suffering helps us grow, but why must it be so intense? So relentless? Why can't we learn these lessons without so much pain?"

Kalan joined them, his energy steady and grounding. "Suffering is not meant to punish, Arya. It is a tool—a powerful one, yes, but also one that brings the soul to its deepest truth. Without darkness, the light would not be as clear. Without hardship, the soul would not stretch beyond its limits."

Zafira's light shimmered gently as she spoke. "Pain has a way of bringing us back to ourselves, of breaking through the illusions that the physical world creates. It strips away the superficial, the temporary, and forces us to confront what truly matters. In moments of suffering, the soul has the opportunity to remember its divine nature."

Arya listened, feeling the truth of their words, but the concept still weighed heavy on her heart. She had experienced many lives where pain seemed overwhelming—where suffering had left her broken and disconnected. How could she embrace suffering when, in her past lives, it had often led her into fear and isolation?

"But what if I don't grow through the suffering?" Arya asked, her voice filled with uncertainty. "What if the pain is too much, and I lose myself in it again?"

Kalan's energy grew stronger, grounding Arya in its warmth. "Suffering is not about being strong in the face of pain, Arya. It's about surrendering to the lesson beneath it. When you resist suffering, when you try to fight it or control it, that's when it overwhelms you. But when you can find acceptance in the midst of it, when you trust that it's there to teach you, it loses its power to control you."

Arya closed her eyes, feeling the depth of Kalan's words. She had resisted suffering in many of her past lives—fought against it, feared it, and in doing so, had let it shape her in ways that deepened her pain. But now, here in this place of understanding, she began to see that the lesson wasn't in the suffering itself—it was in her response to it. If she could accept it, embrace it, and trust that it was guiding her toward something greater, perhaps she could find peace within it.

Lessons of Compassion Through Suffering

Zafira's light glowed more intensely now, as if reflecting Arya's growing understanding. "You will find that suffering, more than any other experience, opens the heart. It is often in our deepest moments of pain that we learn the most profound lessons of compassion, empathy, and connection. When you have suffered, you are able to recognize the suffering in others. It teaches you to love, not in spite of the pain, but because of it."

A vision began to form around Arya, a memory from one of her past lives. She saw herself as a young woman in a small village, struggling to care for her sick child. In that life, she had been filled with anger and frustration, railing against the injustice of her situation. She had felt helpless, and in her helplessness, had turned inward, closing herself off from the world.

But then, in the vision, something changed. Arya saw herself at the bedside of another sick child, this one not her own. Despite her pain, despite her anger, she had reached out to help, offering comfort to a grieving mother who had no one else to turn to. In that moment, Arya had experienced a deep sense of connection—a recognition that her own suffering was not unique, that others around her were facing the same challenges, the same heartache. And in reaching out to help, she had found a sense of peace, a purpose beyond her own pain.

"This is what suffering teaches us," Zafira said softly. "It breaks down the walls of separation. It reminds us that we are all connected, that we are all part of the same journey. When you can open your heart to others, even in the midst of your own pain, you transcend the suffering. You transform it into love."

Arya watched the vision with new eyes, understanding now what she had missed in that lifetime. She had been so focused on her own pain that she hadn't seen the opportunities for connection and compassion that it had brought her. But in that one moment, when she had reached out to help another, she had glimpsed the true purpose of her suffering.

"I see it now," Arya said quietly. "Suffering isn't just about my own growth. It's about how I can use that experience to help others. It's about connection."

Kalan's energy pulsed with approval. "Yes, Arya. When you suffer, you are given the chance to open your heart wider, to feel more deeply, and to understand the struggles of others. It is through suffering that you develop the qualities of compassion, empathy, and unconditional love."

Arya nodded, feeling a deep sense of peace settle within her. She understood now that suffering was not something to be feared or resisted. It was an opportunity to grow, to connect, and to love more deeply. And in her next life, she would carry this understanding with her, knowing that even in her darkest moments, there was a lesson waiting to be learned.

The Gift of Surrender

As Arya absorbed these lessons, she began to feel a shift within herself. The fear she had carried about suffering, the resistance to pain, began to melt away. She understood now that the key to navigating suffering was not to fight it, but to surrender to it. To trust that, beneath the pain, there was always a deeper purpose—a gift waiting to be revealed.

"Suffering teaches you to surrender," Zafira said, her voice filled with quiet wisdom. "It teaches you that control is an illusion, that the more you try to hold on, the more you suffer. But when you can let go, when you can trust that the universe is guiding you, even in your most painful moments, you find freedom."

Arya thought back to the lives where she had fought against the pain, where she had tried to control her circumstances, to avoid suffering at all costs. In those lives, she had only deepened her suffering, because she had refused to let go. But now, with the clarity of the celestial realms, she saw that the greatest gift suffering could offer was the ability to surrender, to trust that everything was unfolding as it was meant to.

"I will try to remember that," Arya said softly. "I will try to let go, to surrender when the pain comes. I know it won't be easy, but I'll try."

Kalan's presence was strong beside her. "It won't be easy, Arya. But you are not alone in this journey. You will have guides, loved ones, and your own inner strength to help you. And when you forget, when the suffering feels overwhelming, you can always return to this moment, to this understanding. It is never lost to you."

Arya felt a deep sense of gratitude for her guides. She knew that the veil of forgetfulness would descend when she was born, and that these truths might be difficult to remember in the midst of her human experience. But she also knew that she had the strength to face whatever challenges came her way, and that her suffering, no matter how intense, would always carry within it the seeds of growth and transformation.

Preparing for the Challenges Ahead

With a renewed sense of purpose, Arya felt ready to face the challenges that lay ahead in her next life. She knew that suffering would be a part of her journey, but she also knew that she had the tools to navigate it with grace and wisdom. Her soul contract, carefully crafted with the guidance of Zafira and Kalan, would provide the framework for her growth, but it was her response to the challenges that would ultimately determine the depth of her transformation.

"You have chosen a path of growth," Zafira said, her voice filled with love. "It will not be easy, but it will be meaningful. Every moment of suffering, every challenge, will bring you closer to the truth of who you are. And when you look back on your life, you will see that the pain was never in vain. It was always guiding you toward love."

Kalan's light pulsed with strength. "And remember, Arya, that you have the power to transform your suffering. It does not define you. You define how you move through it. With every choice you make, you have the opportunity to rise above the pain, to choose love, and to find peace."

Arya felt a deep sense of peace settle over her. She knew that her next life would be filled with challenges, but she also knew that she had the strength to face them. With Zafira and Kalan by her side, she was ready to embrace the journey, knowing that even in the darkest moments, there was always light waiting to be found.

The Final Words Before the Journey Begins

As Arya prepared to leave the celestial realms and enter her new life on Earth, Zafira and Kalan stood with her, their energies filled with love and support. The time had come for her to take the next step, to cross the threshold from the spiritual realm into the physical world, where the lessons she had chosen would unfold.

"You are ready, Arya," Zafira said softly. "You have the strength, the wisdom, and the love to navigate whatever challenges come your way. Remember what you have learned here. Remember that suffering is not the end—it is the beginning of something greater."

Kalan's presence was strong and steady beside her. "And remember, Arya, that we are always with you. Even when the veil descends, even when you forget, we are here, guiding you, supporting you. You are never alone."

Arya felt a surge of gratitude for her guides, for the wisdom they had shared with her, and for the love that surrounded her. She knew that the road ahead would not be easy, but she also knew that she was ready to face it.

With a deep breath, Arya stepped forward, feeling the pull of the Earth as she prepared to be born. The veil of forgetfulness began to descend, but within her heart, she carried the knowledge that everything she would face—every moment of joy, every moment of suffering—was a part of her soul's journey toward love and understanding.

And so, with her heart full of purpose and her mind clear, Arya crossed the threshold into her new life, ready to embrace the challenges, the lessons, and the growth that awaited her.

Chapter 6: The Veil of Forgetfulness

The Descent Into Forgetfulness

As Arya stood at the threshold between the celestial realms and Earth, she felt a subtle shift in the energy around her. The comforting glow of Zafira and Kalan's presence was still with her, but there was a growing awareness of what lay ahead—the experience of being born into a human body, with all its limitations and challenges. And with that birth would come the most difficult part of her journey: the veil of forgetfulness.

"Tell me again about the veil," Arya asked, her voice filled with both curiosity and concern. "Why do we forget who we truly are when we're born? Why do we lose the memory of this place, of the love and light that surrounds us here?"

Zafira's energy shimmered softly, her light growing warmer. "The veil of forgetfulness is not a punishment, Arya. It is a necessary part of your journey on Earth. When you forget your true nature, it allows you to experience life in a way that feels real, immediate, and full of choice. Without the veil, you would not be able to grow in the same way. You would already know the answers before you had lived the questions."

Arya pondered this for a moment, her mind wrapping around the concept. She had lived many lives before, each one beginning with the same veil descending over her consciousness. In each life, she had forgotten the clarity and wisdom she had gained in the spiritual realms, and she had spent years, sometimes lifetimes, trying to remember who she truly was.

"But what if I never remember?" Arya asked softly, the fear of being lost in the human experience weighing on her heart. "What if I get so caught up in the struggles of Earth that I forget the lessons I've learned here? What if I lose my way?"

Kalan's steady presence surrounded her, grounding her in his strength. "You may forget, Arya. That is the nature of life on Earth. But you will never be completely lost. The signs will always be there—small reminders from your higher self, synchronicities, moments of clarity. Even when you cannot remember this place, your soul will know, deep inside, that it is connected to something greater."

Arya felt a small flicker of comfort, though the idea of losing the connection to her true self still unsettled her. She had experienced moments of deep forgetfulness in her past lives—times when the pain and confusion of the human experience had clouded her vision, leaving her feeling alone and disconnected. How would she navigate that again?

"How do I find my way back when I forget?" Arya asked, her voice filled with quiet determination. "How do I remember the truth when I'm living in a world that feels so far from it?"

Zafira's light brightened as she responded. "The key to remembering, Arya, is to listen to the whispers of your soul. You will not always hear them clearly, but they will be there—in the quiet moments, in the feelings of intuition, in the signs that seem to come from nowhere. Your higher self will always be guiding you, even when you cannot see it. And the more you tune in to those whispers, the more you will begin to remember."

The Purpose of Forgetting

As Arya stood in silence, reflecting on the challenge of navigating life through the veil, she began to understand why it was necessary. Without the veil, without the experience of forgetting, her life on Earth would lack the depth of choice. The human experience, with all its complexity, was designed to help her soul grow by allowing her to make decisions without the constant awareness of her divine nature.

"Earth is a school," Kalan explained, his voice rich with understanding. "It is a place where souls go to learn through experience, not theory. If you remembered everything, if you knew exactly why things happened as they did, there would be no room for growth. The veil allows you to learn through living, through the choices you make in the face of uncertainty. That's what makes the human experience so valuable."

Arya nodded slowly, beginning to see the wisdom in it. She had often wondered, in her past lives, why she couldn't remember the truth of her soul, why the answers seemed so elusive. But now, standing here on the brink of another incarnation, she realized that the forgetting was part of the gift. It allowed her to experience life fully, to face challenges as if for the first time, and to learn the lessons that her soul needed to grow.

"The veil creates the illusion of separation," Zafira said softly. "It makes you feel as though you are alone, disconnected from the greater whole. But that illusion is what drives you to seek connection, to find your way back to the truth. Without that sense of separation, you would never fully understand the beauty of unity. The journey from forgetting to remembering is what brings the deepest growth."

Arya felt the weight of those words. She had lived through many lifetimes of forgetting and remembering, of losing herself in the illusions of the material world only to find her way back to the light. And now, she understood that this cycle was not a flaw in the system—it was the very heart of the human experience.

"But how do I know when I'm on the right path?" Arya asked, her voice filled with quiet determination. "How do I know when I'm moving toward remembering, instead of getting lost in the illusions?"

Kalan's energy pulsed with strength. "You will know by how it feels, Arya. When you are aligned with your higher self, when you are moving toward the truth, you will feel a sense of peace, even in the midst of chaos. You will feel connected, even when the world around you seems disconnected. Trust those feelings. They are your compass, guiding you through the fog of forgetfulness."

Navigating the Illusions of Earth

As Arya stood on the edge of her new life, she thought about the world she was about to enter. Earth was a place of duality—of light and dark, joy and suffering, love and fear. And within that duality, it was easy to become lost, to forget the deeper truths of the soul. The human experience, with its dense energy and physical limitations, often clouded the clarity that Arya felt so strongly in the celestial realms.

"Earth is full of illusions," Zafira said gently. "The illusion of separation, the illusion of fear, the illusion that you are small and powerless. But these are just that—illusions. They are not the truth. The truth is that you are always connected, always powerful, always loved. The challenge is to see through the illusions, to remember the truth even when it seems hidden."

A vision began to form before Arya, showing her the life she was about to enter. She saw herself as a child, growing up in a world that seemed filled with limitations. There would be moments of fear, moments of doubt, moments when the illusion of separation would feel overwhelming. But she also saw moments of light—moments when she would remember, even for just a second, that she was more than her human form. She would feel the pull of her soul, the quiet whispers of her guides, and the deep knowing that she was connected to something greater.

"You will face challenges, Arya," Kalan said, his voice steady and grounding. "But those challenges are not there to defeat you. They are there to help you grow, to push you beyond the limitations of the physical world and into the truth of your soul. Each time you face a challenge, you will have the opportunity to see through the illusion, to remember who you really are."

Arya watched the vision unfold, seeing herself navigating the highs and lows of the human experience. She saw moments of joy and connection, moments of love and laughter. But she also saw moments of pain and struggle, times when the veil of forgetfulness would make it difficult to see the light. And yet, even in those darkest moments, she knew that there was always a way back to the truth.

"I'm afraid of getting lost in the illusion," Arya admitted, her voice filled with vulnerability. "I've been lost before, in other lives. How do I stay connected to the truth when the illusions are so powerful?"

Zafira's light shimmered softly as she responded. "You stay connected by cultivating awareness, Arya. By taking time to quiet your mind, to listen to the whispers of your soul. Meditation, prayer, reflection—these are all tools that will help you pierce through the veil. And when you feel disconnected, when the illusions feel too strong, remember to trust the process. You are never truly lost. You are always on your way back to yourself."

Synchronicity and Signs from the Universe

As Arya absorbed the wisdom of her guides, she began to feel a sense of peace settle within her. She understood now that the veil of forgetfulness was not something to fear, but something to work with. It was a part of the human experience that allowed for growth, for the unfolding of her soul's purpose. And while she might forget the full truth of who she was, she knew that there would always be signs to guide her back.

"Synchronicity will be one of your greatest allies," Zafira said, her voice filled with warmth. "When you are aligned with your higher self, the universe will respond. You will experience moments of synchronicity—those seemingly coincidental events that feel too perfect to be random. These are signs from the universe, reminders that you are on the right path."

Arya thought about the moments of synchronicity she had experienced in her past lives—the unexpected encounters, the moments when everything seemed to fall into place as if guided by an unseen hand. She remembered the feeling of being in the flow, of knowing deep in her soul that she was exactly where she was meant to be.

"Pay attention to those moments," Kalan said. "They are the universe's way of communicating with you, of reminding you that you are not alone. When you experience synchronicity, take it as a sign that you are in alignment with your soul's purpose. And when you don't experience it, use that as a signal to pause, reflect, and reconnect with your higher self."

Arya nodded, feeling a sense of comfort in the knowledge that the universe would always be communicating with her, even when she couldn't hear it clearly. The signs would be there, subtle but persistent, guiding her through the fog of forgetfulness and back to the truth of her soul.

The Choice to Remember

As the energy around Arya began to shift, signaling that the time for her descent into her new life was drawing near, she felt a deep sense of resolve. She understood now that forgetting was not a failure—it was part of the journey. And while the veil of forgetfulness would obscure her memories of the spiritual realms, it would also give her the opportunity to remember, to choose her path with intention and awareness.

"You will always have the choice to remember," Zafira said softly. "Even in the darkest moments, when the illusions seem overwhelming, you can choose to reconnect with your soul. It may not always be easy, but the choice is always there. And with each choice, you will strengthen your connection to the truth."

Kalan's energy pulsed with strength beside her. "You have prepared well for this life, Arya. You have the tools, the wisdom, and the love to navigate whatever challenges come your way. And when the veil of forgetfulness feels heavy, remember that it is not permanent. It is only a layer, a thin veil that can be pierced by the light of your awareness."

Arya took a deep breath, feeling the weight of her upcoming journey, but also the excitement that came with the opportunity for growth. She knew that this life would be filled with moments of both forgetting and remembering, of challenges and triumphs. And she knew that, no matter how thick the veil seemed, she had the strength to find her way back to the truth.

"I will remember," Arya said, her voice filled with quiet determination. "Even when I forget, I will find my way back."

Zafira and Kalan's lights shimmered brightly in response, their energies filled with love and support.

"And we will be with you," Zafira said softly. "Always."

With that, Arya felt the final shift in the energy around her, signaling that the time had come for her descent into her new life. The veil of forgetfulness began to descend, gently but unmistakably, obscuring the clarity of the celestial realms. But within her heart, Arya carried the truth—the knowledge that she was never alone, that the signs would always be there, and that no matter how far she wandered, she would always have the choice to remember.

And so, with the love of her guides surrounding her, Arya stepped forward into the unknown, ready to embrace the journey that lay ahead.

Chapter 7: The Choice of Parents

The Significance of Family in the Soul's Journey

As Arya stood in the ethereal plane, still feeling the quiet hum of the universe's vibrations, her guides Zafira and Kalan prepared her for the next major decision in her soul contract. Arya's new life on Earth was beginning to take shape, but now she had to choose her entry point into that life—the family into which she would be born.

Zafira's light shimmered softly as she approached Arya. "The family you choose, Arya, will play a significant role in your journey. The relationships you form with them will help shape the person you become. They will be your first teachers, your first reflections, and they will influence the path you take in your early years."

Arya knew that family was one of the most important aspects of a human life. In her past incarnations, her family had often been the source of both her greatest joys and her deepest wounds. Through them, she had learned lessons about love, loyalty, and forgiveness, but also about conflict, abandonment, and loss.

Kalan stepped forward, his presence strong and grounding. "This time, Arya, the family you choose will help you explore the lessons of unconditional love, but they will also present challenges. Remember, your choice is not about finding the perfect family, but the family that will best help you grow."

A vision began to unfold before Arya, showing her different families, each one carrying its own energy, its own dynamic. Some families radiated warmth and love, while others seemed more distant, with lessons of independence and resilience woven into their fabric.

"Each family carries a unique set of energies," Zafira explained. "Some will support you unconditionally, while others will challenge you to find your strength and identity. Both paths are valuable. What matters is what your soul is ready to learn."

Arya gazed at the families, each one representing a different path, a different set of lessons. She felt a deep sense of responsibility as she contemplated this choice. The family she chose would shape her early experiences, laying the foundation for her entire life. It was a decision that would affect not only her but also the souls of those she chose as her parents, siblings, and extended family members.

Meeting the Souls of Her Future Family

As Arya watched the vision of the families, she felt a soft tug in her consciousness—a sense of recognition that drew her toward one particular family. The energy of this family felt both familiar and challenging, filled with love but also moments of conflict and growth. Arya focused her attention on them, and slowly, the souls of her future family began to appear before her.

The first to step forward was a woman, her energy warm and radiant. Arya immediately recognized her as the soul who would be her mother in the next life. This soul carried with her the vibration of deep compassion, but also a quiet sadness, as if she had known loss in many lives before this one. Arya could feel that her mother's love would be a guiding force in her life, but she would also face challenges in learning to love herself.

"She will be your greatest teacher in this life," Zafira said softly. "Her love for you will be strong, but it will also be tied to her own struggles with self-worth. Through her, you will learn the balance between receiving love and giving love freely, without condition."

Arya felt a deep sense of connection to this soul. She had known her in previous lives, but in those lives, their relationship had been different—sometimes as sisters, sometimes as friends, but always marked by a deep bond. This time, they would take on the roles of mother and daughter, a relationship that would carry with it new lessons.

Next, a second figure stepped forward, his energy steady but distant. Arya immediately recognized this soul as the man who would be her father. His presence was calm, but there was a barrier around him, a sense of emotional distance that Arya could feel even in this moment.

"Your father will challenge you to find love within yourself," Kalan explained. "His emotional distance will push you to seek validation from within, rather than looking for it in others. It will be a difficult lesson, but an important one. Through him, you will learn independence, resilience, and the power of self-love."

Arya felt a mixture of emotions as she considered this soul. His presence would be one of her greatest challenges in this life. He would be there, physically present, but emotionally distant, and Arya knew that his love for her, though real, would be hard for him to express. It would be up to her to find peace in this dynamic, to learn that love didn't always need to come in the way she expected.

Finally, two more souls appeared before her. These would be her siblings—one older and one younger. The older sibling, a boy with a sharp, energetic presence, would challenge her throughout her childhood. Arya could sense the competitive energy that would define their relationship, but she also knew that beneath the rivalry, there was a deep love that would help both of them grow.

The younger sibling, a girl with a gentle, quiet presence, would look up to Arya throughout their childhood. Arya could feel that she would take on a nurturing role with her younger sibling, offering protection and guidance. But she also knew that this relationship would teach her about boundaries and the importance of allowing others to find their own way.

"This family is not perfect, Arya," Zafira said softly. "But they are perfect for you. Through them, you will learn the lessons of love, independence, and resilience that your soul has chosen to experience in this lifetime."

The Soul Contracts with Her Parents

As Arya stood before the souls of her future family, she felt a deep sense of recognition. These were souls she had traveled with through many lifetimes, and now, once again, they were coming together to help each other grow. Each one had agreed to play a specific role in her life, just as she had agreed to play a role in theirs.

"You have traveled with these souls before," Zafira said gently. "In this lifetime, you have chosen to meet again, to help each other learn the lessons that your souls have set out to experience. Each of you has created a contract, an agreement, to fulfill certain roles in each other's lives."

Arya could feel the weight of these soul contracts. She knew that her mother would love her deeply, but she would also need to learn how to love herself. Her father would challenge her to find strength and self-worth from within, and her siblings would teach her about rivalry, protection, and the delicate balance of independence and connection.

"These contracts are not fixed," Kalan reminded her. "They are guides, but they allow for free will. How you respond to these relationships, how you choose to navigate the challenges and the joys, is up to you. Each of you has agreed to help each other grow, but the path you take together will be shaped by the choices you make."

Arya nodded, feeling a deep sense of responsibility. These souls, her future family, were not just random people—each one had chosen to be a part of her journey, just as she had chosen to be a part of theirs. The bonds they would form, the love they would share, and the challenges they would face together were all part of a larger plan, designed to help each of them evolve.

"Are you ready to choose them?" Zafira asked softly, her light surrounding Arya in warmth.

Arya took a deep breath, feeling the energy of her future family envelop her. She knew that the path ahead would not always be easy, but she also knew that these souls would help her learn the lessons she had chosen for this life.

"I am ready," Arya said, her voice filled with quiet determination. "I choose them."

The Lessons of Family and Karma

As Arya made her choice, the energy around her shifted, solidifying the soul contracts between her and her future family. The decision had been made, and now the threads of karma that bound them together began to glow softly, illuminating the lessons that would unfold in their lives.

"Each relationship you form in this life is tied to the energy of karma," Zafira explained. "The love, the challenges, the conflicts—all of it is part of the karmic balance between souls. You have shared lifetimes with these souls before, and now, once again, you will help each other learn and grow."

Arya understood now that her family relationships were not just about this one lifetime—they were part of a much larger tapestry that spanned many incarnations. In some lives, her mother had been her sister, her father her rival, and her siblings had taken on various roles, each one helping her learn different aspects of love, forgiveness, and growth. This time, the dynamics would be different, but the purpose would remain the same.

"You will have the opportunity to heal old wounds with these souls," Kalan said. "In past lives, there may have been unresolved conflicts, unspoken words, or unhealed pain. In this life, you will have the chance to resolve those karmic ties, to bring balance to your relationships and to learn the lessons of love and forgiveness."

Arya felt the weight of these karmic ties, but she also felt a deep sense of purpose. She knew that this life would be her opportunity to heal, to break free from old patterns, and to create new dynamics that were based on love and understanding.

"Remember, Arya," Zafira said softly, "that the challenges you face with your family are not meant to harm you. They are there to help you grow. When you face conflict, when you feel misunderstood or unloved, remember that these moments are opportunities for healing. Every challenge is a chance to choose love, to choose forgiveness, and to bring balance to your relationships."

Arya nodded, feeling a sense of peace settle within her. She knew that her family would not always be easy to navigate, but she also knew that each challenge would bring her closer to the truth of who she was and the lessons she had chosen to learn.

Final Preparations Before Birth

With her family chosen and the soul contracts in place, Arya felt a deep sense of readiness. She had made the important decisions that would shape her early life, and now, all that remained was the final preparation for her descent into the physical world.

Zafira and Kalan stood beside her, their energies filled with love and support. The time for her birth was drawing near, and Arya could feel the pull of Earth growing stronger. The dense vibrations of the material world were beginning to call her, signaling that it was time to take the next step in her soul's journey.

"You are ready, Arya," Zafira said softly. "You have chosen well, and now you are prepared to enter your new life. Remember the lessons you have learned here, and trust that even when the veil of forgetfulness descends, your soul will guide you. You are never alone."

Kalan's presence was strong and steady beside her. "And remember that we are always with you, even when you cannot see or hear us. You will feel our guidance in the moments of stillness, in the signs and synchronicities that will appear throughout your life. Trust those moments, and trust yourself."

Arya felt a deep sense of gratitude for her guides, for the wisdom they had shared with her, and for the love that surrounded her. She knew that the road ahead would be filled with both joy and challenges, but she also knew that she was ready.

"I am ready," Arya said, her voice filled with quiet determination. "I am ready to be born."

And with those final words, Arya felt the energy of the celestial realms begin to shift, gently pulling her toward the Earth. The veil of forgetfulness began to descend, obscuring the clarity of the spiritual realms, but within her heart, Arya carried the knowledge that she had chosen this path, that her family would help her grow, and that she had the strength to navigate whatever challenges lay ahead.

With her heart full of purpose and her mind clear, Arya stepped forward into the physical world, ready to begin the next chapter of her soul's journey.

Chapter 8: Choosing Life's Challenges

The Purpose of Challenges

As the energy of the celestial realms gently hummed around Arya, she stood still, her thoughts filled with the weight of the choices yet to be made. She had chosen her family—her first teachers and mirrors on Earth—but now came another crucial decision. It was time to select the challenges she would face, the trials that would push her to grow and evolve.

Zafira stood by her side, her soft light pulsing gently, filling the space around them with warmth and reassurance. "The challenges you choose, Arya, will not be random. Each one will be carefully selected to help you grow in the ways your soul desires. It is through difficulty that the soul learns resilience, compassion, and wisdom."

Arya knew this truth well. In her past lives, she had faced many trials—illness, betrayal, loss, and heartbreak—and each one had shaped her, refined her. Yet in the heat of those challenges, she had often wondered why they were necessary, why life had to be so hard. Now, from the vantage point of the spiritual realm, she understood: each challenge had been an opportunity, a doorway to deeper understanding.

"But how do I know which challenges to choose?" Arya asked, her voice filled with quiet uncertainty. "What if I pick something too difficult? What if I can't handle it?"

Kalan's presence, strong and steady, moved closer. His energy wrapped around Arya, grounding her in a sense of calm. "The challenges you face will never be more than you can bear, Arya. You will always have the strength to navigate them, even when they feel overwhelming. And remember, each challenge will come with the support of those around you—your guides, your higher self, and the people you meet along the way."

A vision began to form before Arya, showing the different challenges she could choose. Some were physical—illness, injury, or physical limitation. Others were emotional—loss, betrayal, the pain of heartbreak. And still others were mental—confusion, doubt, the struggle to find her way through the complexity of life.

Facing the Challenges of Loss

As Arya gazed at the swirling possibilities, one vision stood out from the rest. She saw herself standing in a room filled with quiet, heavy grief. A loved one had passed, and the weight of loss pressed down on her like a leaden blanket. She felt the sharp, aching pain in her chest, the feeling of being left behind. It was a deep, raw wound, one that would take time to heal.

Zafira stepped forward, her energy softening as she saw the sorrow on Arya's face. "Loss is one of the greatest teachers," she said gently. "It teaches you about impermanence, about letting go. Through loss, you will learn to cherish the moments of connection you have, to love deeply without clinging, and to find peace even when the people you love are no longer with you."

Arya's heart ached as she watched the vision of herself moving through grief. She had known loss in her past lives—parents, lovers, children—and each time, it had broken her open in ways she hadn't expected. But she had also grown through those losses. They had taught her about the depth of love, about the fragility of life, and about the strength that comes from continuing on even when everything seemed to fall apart.

"I know this lesson," Arya said quietly. "But it never gets easier."

"It is not meant to be easy," Kalan said, his voice filled with strength. "But it is meant to transform you. Loss teaches you that nothing in the physical world is permanent, and yet love—the essence of the soul—never truly dies. Through the experience of loss, you will learn to love without attachment, to find connection even in separation."

Arya nodded, her heart heavy but resolute. She knew that loss would be a part of her life on Earth, just as it had been in her past incarnations. But this time, she was determined to face it with more awareness, to use the pain as a tool for growth rather than letting it consume her.

Choosing Lessons of Betrayal and Forgiveness

As the vision of loss faded, another vision emerged. This time, Arya saw herself standing face to face with someone she trusted—a close friend or lover. But there was pain in the air between them, a sense of betrayal. She could feel the sharp sting of betrayal in her heart, the anger and disbelief that followed. The person she had trusted had broken that trust, and the wound ran deep.

Arya flinched as she watched the vision unfold, feeling the familiar pang of betrayal. In her past lives, betrayal had been one of the hardest lessons to learn. It had left scars on her soul, deep wounds that had taken lifetimes to heal.

"Betrayal is a powerful teacher," Zafira said gently. "It shows you the parts of yourself that are still attached to control, to expectations. When you are betrayed, you are given the opportunity to release those attachments, to find strength within yourself, and to practice forgiveness."

Arya watched herself in the vision, her heart torn between anger and sorrow. She saw the moment when she had the choice to hold onto the bitterness or to forgive. In her past lives, she had often struggled with forgiveness, finding it hard to let go of the pain others had caused her. But she also knew that forgiveness was one of the most powerful forces in the universe—it had the ability to heal not just her, but the person who had wronged her.

"Forgiveness is not about condoning the harm done to you," Kalan said, his voice firm. "It is about freeing yourself from the chains of resentment. When you forgive, you are not saying that what happened was acceptable. You are saying that you will no longer allow it to control you. You are choosing peace over pain."

Arya felt the weight of those words settle deep within her. She knew that betrayal would be one of the challenges she would face in her next life, and she also knew that forgiveness would be one of the greatest lessons she would have to learn. It would not be easy, but she was ready to face it.

The Challenge of Illness and Physical Limitation

As the vision of betrayal faded, Arya saw a new challenge appear before her. This time, she was lying in a bed, her body weak and frail. She felt the weight of illness pressing down on her, limiting her movement, her energy, her ability to engage fully with the world around her. The pain was not just physical—it was emotional, a deep sense of helplessness that came with being unable to control her own body.

Arya watched the vision with a sense of quiet resignation. Illness had been a part of her past lives as well, and it had always been a difficult challenge to face. The limitations it placed on her had often left her feeling frustrated and powerless.

"Illness is one of the most profound teachers," Zafira said softly. "It forces you to slow down, to turn inward, and to confront the parts of yourself that are not tied to the physical body. Through illness, you will learn that you are more than your body, that your worth and value are not tied to your physical abilities."

Kalan's presence was strong beside her. "Illness also teaches you about surrender. When you are ill, you are faced with the limits of your control. You must learn to let go, to trust that even when your body is weak, your spirit remains strong. It is a lesson in patience, in resilience, and in the power of the soul to transcend the physical."

Arya nodded, feeling the truth of their words. Illness would be a challenge she would face in her next life, and though it frightened her, she knew it would also bring her closer to the deeper truth of who she was—a soul, not a body.

Embracing the Path of Growth

As Arya stood in the ethereal plane, watching the visions of her future life unfold, she felt a deep sense of both trepidation and purpose. The challenges she had chosen—loss, betrayal, illness—were not easy ones. They would push her to her limits, testing her resilience, her strength, and her ability to love and forgive. But she also knew that these challenges were the key to her soul's growth.

"You have chosen well," Zafira said softly. "These challenges will not break you, Arya. They will refine you. They will help you become the person your soul is meant to be."

Kalan's presence was strong and reassuring beside her. "And remember, Arya, that you are never alone. Even in the darkest moments, when the challenges feel overwhelming, we will be with you. Your higher self will always guide you, and you will have the strength to face whatever comes your way."

Arya took a deep breath, feeling the weight of her choices settle within her. She knew that the path ahead would not be easy, but she also knew that she had the strength, the wisdom, and the love to navigate it. With her challenges chosen and her soul contract complete, she was ready to step into her new life.

"I am ready," Arya said, her voice filled with quiet determination. "I am ready to grow."

And with that, the energy of the celestial realms began to shift once more, preparing Arya for her descent into the physical world. The challenges she had chosen were waiting for her, but so too were the lessons, the growth, and the love that would shape her journey.

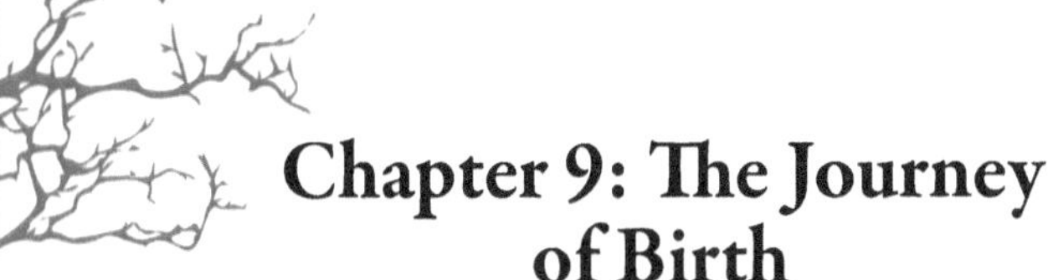

Chapter 9: The Journey
of Birth

The Descent into Earth

The time had come. Arya could feel the pull of Earth growing stronger, the dense vibrations of the material world calling to her. The energy of the celestial realms around her began to shift, swirling with anticipation as she prepared for the most profound transition a soul can make—the journey of birth.

Zafira and Kalan stood with her, their presence filled with love and support. Though the path ahead would take Arya far from the clarity and light of the spiritual realms, she knew that her guides would be with her, even if she couldn't always sense them. In moments of stillness, in flashes of intuition, she would remember.

"Are you ready, Arya?" Zafira asked, her voice soft but filled with deep knowing.

Arya's heart swelled with a mixture of emotions—excitement, nervousness, and a quiet determination. She had prepared for this moment, chosen her family, her challenges, and the lessons that would shape her life. Now, it was time to step into the unknown.

"I am ready," Arya said, her voice steady.

As the words left her, the energy around her began to vibrate more intensely, signaling the start of her descent. Arya could feel the veil of forgetfulness creeping closer, a thin but impenetrable layer that would soon cloud her memories of the spiritual realms. She would forget her guides, her past lives, and the soul contract she had so carefully crafted. But deep within her soul, the truth would remain, waiting to be remembered.

Passing Through the Veil

The veil of forgetfulness began to descend more fully now, wrapping itself around Arya like a heavy mist. It was not sudden, but gradual, a soft clouding of her awareness. The clarity of the celestial realms, once so sharp and vibrant, began to fade, replaced by the hazy sensation of the physical world.

Arya felt herself being pulled downward, her consciousness shifting from the vastness of the spiritual plane to the small, contained space of her new body. It was an odd sensation, this narrowing of awareness. Where once she had been expansive, limitless, now she felt the confines of the human form closing in around her. Her senses began to dull, and with each passing moment, the connection to the higher realms grew fainter.

Zafira's voice echoed gently in her consciousness, though it was distant now, like a whisper carried on the wind. "You are never alone, Arya. Even when you forget, we are always with you."

Arya tried to hold onto Zafira's words, but they slipped away as the veil of forgetfulness thickened. Her connection to the spiritual world dimmed, and she could feel the weight of the physical world pressing down on her.

For a brief moment, a sense of panic welled up inside her. The vastness of the celestial realms had been so comforting, so filled with light and love. How would she find her way in this new, limited existence? How would she remember the truth when everything around her felt so dense, so disconnected?

But then, as quickly as the panic rose, it subsided. Arya remembered the lessons she had learned in the spiritual realms. She remembered that the path of forgetting was not a mistake—it was part of the journey. She had chosen this life, these challenges, and she had the strength to navigate them.

The First Breath

As Arya moved deeper into the physical realm, she could feel the sensation of her new body forming around her. It was strange and unfamiliar, this new vessel, but it was also a source of great potential. Through this body, she would experience life in ways that were impossible in the spiritual realm. She would feel, touch, taste, and love in ways that only a human could.

Her consciousness, now fully tied to the physical world, began to settle into her new form. She was an infant, small and fragile, but filled with the infinite potential of a soul on the verge of a great journey. As she took her first breath, the veil of forgetfulness closed completely around her, leaving her fully immersed in the human experience.

In that moment, Arya forgot everything—the celestial realms, her guides, the soul contract she had carefully crafted. All that remained was the present moment, the sensation of being alive in a new body, in a new world. Her senses, once dull and unfamiliar, began to awaken, slowly taking in the world around her.

The first thing she felt was warmth—the warmth of her mother's arms as they wrapped around her, holding her close. It was a sensation of safety, of love, though Arya could not yet name it. The connection she felt to her mother was deep and immediate, as if their souls recognized each other even through the veil of forgetfulness. This was the woman who would guide her through the early years of her life, the one who would teach her about love, compassion, and resilience.

Though Arya could not remember the conversations she had shared with her guides in the celestial realms, the connection she felt with her mother brought her a sense of peace. She was where she needed to be.

The Awakening of Senses

As Arya's body adjusted to the physical world, her senses slowly began to come online. The sounds around her were muffled, distant, like echoes in a vast canyon. But as the moments passed, the sounds sharpened. She could hear the gentle murmur of voices, the soft hum of life around her.

Her eyes, still blurry, caught glimpses of light and shadow, shapes moving in and out of her field of vision. Everything was new, unfamiliar, but there was a sense of curiosity growing within her. Even through the veil, her soul recognized the beauty and mystery of the physical world.

Her tiny fingers, curled into fists, slowly unfurled, reaching out into the air as if searching for something to hold onto. The sensation of touch was new and strange, but it also carried with it a sense of connection to the world around her.

In those first moments, Arya didn't understand what was happening. Her mind, still clouded by the veil of forgetfulness, couldn't make sense of the world she had entered. But her soul, deep within, was filled with a quiet knowing. She had chosen this life, this body, these experiences. And though the journey ahead would be filled with challenges, it would also be filled with moments of profound beauty, connection, and growth.

The Soul's Quiet Knowing

Though Arya was now fully immersed in the physical world, the truth of her soul remained quietly nestled within her. The veil of forgetfulness had done its work, obscuring her memories of the spiritual realms, but it could not erase the essence of who she was.

Deep within her, beneath the layers of human experience that were already beginning to form, Arya's soul remained connected to the higher realms. It was a connection she would rediscover over the course of her life, in moments of stillness, in moments of love, and in moments of quiet reflection. Though she would forget, she would also remember.

For now, Arya was content to simply exist in this new world. Her body, her senses, her mind—everything was new, everything was an experience waiting to unfold. She had forgotten the vastness of the spiritual realms, but she had also gained something in return: the opportunity to grow, to learn, and to discover the truth of her soul in the physical world.

As her mother's arms held her close, Arya felt a sense of peace settle over her. She was exactly where she needed to be. The journey had begun.

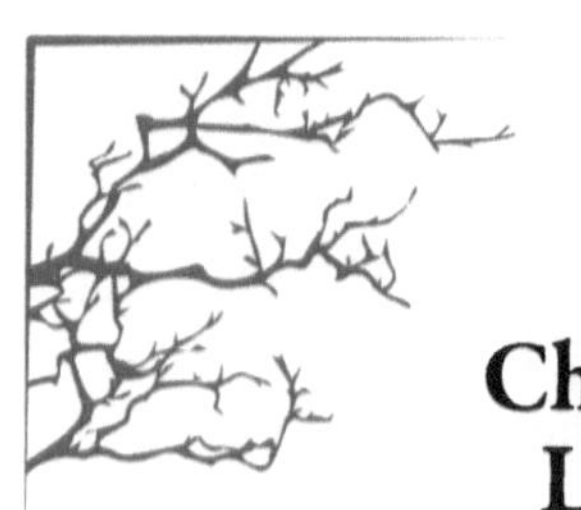

Chapter 10: Early Lessons of Life

The Bond with Her Mother

In the first few years of Arya's life, the world was small—comprised mostly of the warmth of her mother's arms, the comforting rhythm of her heartbeat, and the soft glow of sunlight filtering through the windows of her childhood home. The simplicity of these early moments was profound, yet Arya's soul, tucked beneath the layers of her new existence, was absorbing more than her mind could comprehend.

Her mother was her first teacher, not through words, but through the quiet lessons of love and nurture. Every time her mother cradled her, fed her, or soothed her cries, Arya learned about trust and connection. The bond between them was deep, forged long before Arya's birth, and though she could not remember their past lives together, the love between them carried the unmistakable imprint of souls who had traveled this path before.

Even through the veil of forgetfulness, Arya could feel the depth of her mother's love. It was a love that would guide her through the early years of her life, teaching her the foundational lessons of compassion and empathy. But beneath that love, there was also a quiet sadness that Arya couldn't quite understand yet—a sadness that her mother carried like a hidden weight.

In moments of stillness, when Arya lay curled up in her mother's lap, she could feel that sadness, like a distant echo. It was something her mother had carried with her from past lives, unresolved and unspoken.

Though Arya was too young to name it, her soul recognized it. In time, she would come to understand that part of her journey would involve helping her mother heal that pain.

The Awakening of Curiosity

As Arya grew, so did her awareness of the world around her. The once small, contained space of her early life began to expand, revealing a world filled with wonder and mystery. Every new sensation, every new discovery was a lesson—her fingers tracing the softness of a blanket, the coolness of a breeze against her skin, the sound of her father's voice resonating through the room.

With each new experience, Arya's curiosity blossomed. The world was a puzzle waiting to be explored, and though her mind was still too young to understand the complexities of life, her soul thrived in the simple joy of discovery.

Her father's presence in her life was steady, though often distant. He was a quiet man, reserved in his affections, but his love for Arya was evident in the small things—building her a wooden toy, carrying her on his shoulders, or sitting beside her as she explored her growing collection of storybooks.

Yet, even in these early years, Arya could feel the emotional distance that separated them. She longed for more from him—more affection, more connection—but his love, though real, was restrained. Her soul recognized this distance as one of the lessons she had chosen: to learn how to find love within herself, rather than relying on it from others.

The First Glimpse of Independence

Around the age of four, Arya began to assert her independence, taking small steps away from the protective cocoon of her mother's embrace and into the wider world. These early moments of separation were both thrilling and unsettling. On the one hand, Arya delighted in the newfound freedom—running through the garden, climbing trees, exploring the small world beyond her home. On the other hand, there was a growing awareness that the world was not as safe or as predictable as it seemed.

Her older brother, with his sharp energy and competitive spirit, often challenged her during these early years. Their relationship, marked by a mixture of rivalry and affection, pushed Arya to test her boundaries, to stand up for herself, and to develop a sense of self separate from her family.

Though their playful squabbles often left Arya frustrated, they also taught her about resilience. Her brother's teasing, while sometimes hurtful, forced her to look inward, to find strength and confidence in who she was. The lessons of independence were subtle but powerful. Each time Arya fell, each time she was pushed, she learned how to get back up, how to navigate the challenges that life presented with grace and determination.

The Bond with Her Younger Sister

The dynamic with her younger sister was entirely different. From the moment her sister was born, Arya felt an innate sense of protectiveness. The baby girl, small and fragile, looked up to Arya with wide, trusting eyes, and Arya responded to that trust with love and care. Though only a few years older, Arya quickly took on the role of protector, guiding her younger sister through the early stages of childhood with a gentle hand.

Their bond was quiet but strong, a thread of love that wove itself through their days together. Arya's younger sister adored her, following her wherever she went, mimicking her every move. In those early years, Arya discovered the delicate balance between nurturing and independence. Her role as the older sibling gave her a sense of responsibility, but it also taught her the importance of allowing her sister to find her own way.

Through this relationship, Arya learned her first lessons in love without attachment. She loved her sister deeply, but she also understood that her role was not to control or dictate her sister's path—it was to support and guide her, while allowing her the freedom to grow into her own person.

The Soul's First Stirring of Memory

As the years passed and Arya moved through the early stages of childhood, there were moments—quiet, fleeting moments—when something deeper stirred within her. These moments often came during times of stillness, when Arya was alone, sitting beneath the shade of a tree or watching the clouds drift lazily across the sky.

In those moments, a sense of familiarity would wash over her, as if she had lived these scenes before, though she couldn't quite place when or where. It was a feeling, more than a memory—a soft stirring in her heart that reminded her of something beyond the physical world, something vast and infinite.

Once, while lying in bed and staring up at the ceiling, Arya felt a sudden wave of longing wash over her—a longing for a place she couldn't remember, a place filled with light and peace. The feeling passed as quickly as it came, but it left an imprint on her heart, a quiet knowing that there was more to her existence than what she could see with her eyes.

These stirrings were the first whispers of her soul, the first hints that her connection to the higher realms was still there, buried beneath the layers of human experience. Though she had forgotten the details of her soul's journey, the essence of who she was remained intact, waiting patiently for her to remember.

The Subtle Lessons of Love and Patience

As Arya's early years unfolded, she began to understand the subtle lessons life was offering her. Love, she learned, was not always expressed in the ways she expected. Her mother's love was soft, unconditional, and ever-present, while her father's love was quiet and reserved, often hidden beneath layers of silence. Her siblings each expressed their love in different ways—her brother through playful competition, her sister through unwavering admiration.

Through these early relationships, Arya began to develop a deeper understanding of patience. She learned that love was not something to be demanded or expected—it was something that flowed naturally, in its own time, in its own way. Sometimes it was loud and exuberant, and other times it was quiet and subtle, but it was always there, woven into the fabric of her life.

Though she was still young, Arya's soul was beginning to recognize the lessons it had chosen for this life. Each relationship, each moment of connection, was a part of the larger plan, designed to help her grow and evolve. The seeds of understanding were being planted, and in time, they would blossom into deeper awareness.

Chapter 11: The First Tests of Karma

The First Glimpse of Karma in Action

As Arya approached her seventh birthday, the simplicity of her early childhood began to give way to more complex emotions and experiences. Life, which had once been filled with the warmth of family and the joy of exploration, now presented its first real tests. These were not the monumental challenges of adulthood, but small, quiet trials that nonetheless carried the weight of karmic lessons.

The first of these came in the form of conflict with her older brother. Their sibling rivalry, once playful, began to intensify as they grew older. Where before their quarrels had been little more than teasing, now they carried an edge—a sharpness that Arya hadn't noticed before. Her brother, competitive and headstrong, often pushed her beyond her comfort zone, challenging her both physically and emotionally. Arya, for her part, responded with frustration and anger, unsure how to navigate the growing tension between them.

One afternoon, after a particularly heated argument, Arya retreated to her favorite spot beneath the large oak tree in their yard. Her chest ached with a mixture of hurt and confusion. She didn't understand why her brother seemed determined to provoke her, why their once-fun interactions now left her feeling small and powerless.

As she sat beneath the tree, a memory from deep within her soul stirred. It wasn't a clear memory, not something she could recall with her mind, but a feeling—a sense that this conflict with her brother was familiar. It was as if they had been here before, in another life, playing out the same roles, the same tensions.

"Why does he do this?" Arya asked herself, her voice barely a whisper.

Though she didn't yet have the words for it, Arya was beginning to understand the concept of karma. The push and pull between her and her brother was not random; it was part of a much larger pattern, one that had been set in motion long before they were born. This was a test—an opportunity for Arya to learn how to navigate conflict with love rather than anger.

The Struggle with Anger

Arya had always been a sensitive child, quick to feel the emotions of those around her. But as she grew older, she began to notice a new emotion rising within her—anger. It wasn't the playful, fleeting anger of childhood tantrums; it was deeper, more intense. It flared up during arguments with her brother, when she felt misunderstood by her parents, or when something didn't go her way.

At first, Arya didn't know how to handle the anger. It burned inside her, leaving her feeling helpless and out of control. She hated the way it made her feel, but she didn't know how to make it go away. She tried to push it down, to ignore it, but the more she tried to suppress it, the stronger it became.

One evening, after an argument with her father, Arya stormed out of the house and ran to the oak tree. Her chest heaved with frustration, her hands clenched into fists. The argument had been about something small—chores, perhaps, or a rule her father had set—but in that moment, it felt monumental. Her father's calm, distant demeanor only made her angrier. Why couldn't he see how much she was struggling? Why didn't he understand her?

As she sat beneath the tree, Arya's mind raced, replaying the argument over and over. But then, slowly, her anger began to fade, replaced by a quiet sadness. She didn't want to feel this way. She didn't want to be angry all the time. But she didn't know how to stop.

For the first time, Arya wondered if her anger wasn't just about the present moment. Maybe it was something deeper, something she had carried with her from other lives. The thought was unsettling, but it also brought a strange sense of relief. If the anger was part of a larger pattern, then maybe, just maybe, she could find a way to heal it.

Learning the Lesson of Forgiveness

A few days after the argument with her father, Arya found herself alone in the kitchen with her mother. The house was quiet, the soft hum of the evening settling over them. Arya had been thinking a lot about the anger she felt, not just with her father, but with her brother and even herself. She wanted to talk about it, but the words were hard to find.

Her mother, sensing her daughter's inner turmoil, sat down beside her and placed a gentle hand on her shoulder. "What's on your mind, Arya?" she asked softly.

Arya hesitated for a moment before speaking. "Why do I get so angry?" she asked, her voice barely above a whisper. "I don't want to, but I can't help it."

Her mother smiled gently, her eyes filled with understanding. "Anger is a part of life," she said. "We all feel it sometimes. But the important thing is what we do with that anger. It's okay to feel it, but it's also important to learn how to let it go."

Arya looked down at her hands, feeling the weight of her mother's words. "But how do I let it go?" she asked.

Her mother took a deep breath, her expression thoughtful. "Sometimes, the best way to let go of anger is through forgiveness," she said. "Not just forgiving others, but also forgiving yourself. When you forgive, you free yourself from the weight of the anger. It doesn't mean you forget what happened or that it was okay, but it means you're choosing to let go of the pain it caused."

Arya considered her mother's words carefully. She thought about the anger she had felt toward her father, her brother, and even herself. Could she really forgive them? Could she forgive herself?

"It's not easy," her mother continued, "but forgiveness is one of the most powerful things you can do. It's a way to heal, to move forward without carrying the pain with you."

That night, as Arya lay in bed, she thought about what her mother had said. Forgiveness wasn't just about the other person—it was about her. It was about freeing herself from the chains of anger and allowing herself to move forward.

The idea of forgiveness didn't erase the hurt or make everything perfect, but it brought Arya a small sense of peace. Maybe, just maybe, she could start to forgive—not only her father and brother but also herself. And in doing so, she could begin to heal the karmic patterns that had followed her through lifetimes.

The First Lessons of Empathy

As Arya began to explore the idea of forgiveness, another lesson quietly emerged: empathy. She had always been sensitive to the emotions of those around her, but now, as she grew older, she began to understand that empathy was more than just feeling someone else's pain—it was about understanding their experience.

It started with her younger sister. One evening, as they sat together, Arya noticed that her sister seemed unusually quiet. Usually bubbly and full of energy, her sister now sat with her knees pulled up to her chest, her eyes distant.

"What's wrong?" Arya asked softly.

Her sister didn't respond at first, but after a few moments, she whispered, "I just feel lonely sometimes. Like no one really understands me."

Arya felt a pang of sadness in her chest. She had never thought about her sister feeling lonely. To her, her sister had always seemed so full of life, so happy. But now, Arya realized that her sister, too, had her own struggles, her own inner world that wasn't always visible.

For the first time, Arya saw her sister not just as a younger sibling to protect, but as a person with her own emotions, her own pain. And in that moment, Arya felt a deep sense of empathy—a desire to truly understand what her sister was going through, to be there for her in a way that went beyond just being a protector.

"I understand," Arya said quietly, wrapping her arm around her sister. "I feel that way sometimes too. But you're not alone. I'm here."

Her sister looked up at her, a small smile playing at the corners of her lips. "Thanks," she whispered.

In that moment, Arya realized that empathy was one of the most important lessons she could learn. It wasn't just about feeling someone else's pain—it was about being there for them, about offering love and understanding even when she didn't have all the answers.

Awakening to Karmic Patterns

As the months passed, Arya began to notice other patterns emerging in her life—patterns that felt familiar in a way she couldn't quite explain. She noticed how her relationships with her family seemed to follow certain dynamics, how the same conflicts and emotions kept repeating. It was as if the challenges she faced were not new, but echoes of something deeper.

One evening, as Arya sat alone in her room, she felt a quiet stirring within her. It was the same feeling she had experienced beneath the oak tree—a sense that her life, her experiences, were part of something much larger. It was as if she were waking up to the realization that these patterns, these challenges, were part of her karmic journey.

The anger she felt, the conflicts with her brother, the distance from her father—all of it was part of a tapestry that had been woven over many lifetimes. Each thread carried with it the weight of past choices, past actions, and now, in this life, Arya had the opportunity to heal those threads, to create new patterns based on love, forgiveness, and understanding.

For the first time, Arya began to see her life not as a series of random events, but as a carefully orchestrated journey—a journey that her soul had chosen. And with that realization came a sense of empowerment. She was not a victim of her circumstances; she was an active participant in her soul's evolution.

In that quiet moment, Arya made a silent promise to herself: She would face the challenges that life presented her with grace and courage. She would forgive, she would love, and she would do her best to break the karmic patterns that had followed her through lifetimes.

This life was her chance to grow, to heal, and to evolve. And she was ready to embrace it fully.

Chapter 12: The Role of Friendship and Connection

The First True Friend

As Arya grew into her eighth year, the world around her expanded beyond the familiar walls of her home and the comforting presence of her family. School, once just a place for learning letters and numbers, now became the backdrop for new relationships, for connections that would shape the course of her early life. It was in this setting that Arya met someone who would become her first true friend—a girl named Leila.

Leila was different from anyone Arya had ever known. She had a quiet strength about her, a confidence that seemed to radiate from within. While other children vied for attention or sought approval, Leila was content to observe, to listen. She carried herself with a grace that drew Arya to her almost immediately.

It started with small gestures—a shared seat during lunch, a smile exchanged during a difficult math lesson. But soon, Arya and Leila became inseparable. They spent their days together, running through the schoolyard, sharing secrets, and dreaming about the future. In Leila, Arya found a kindred spirit, someone who understood her in a way that no one else seemed to.

For the first time, Arya felt the deep joy of connection outside of her family. Leila wasn't just a friend—she was a mirror, reflecting back to Arya the parts of herself that she had yet to discover. Their friendship felt effortless, natural, as if they had known each other for far longer than their short time together on Earth.

But beneath the joy of their friendship, Arya sensed something deeper—an unspoken connection that went beyond the present moment. It was as if their souls had met before, in lifetimes past, and were now coming together once again to continue a journey they had started long ago.

The Challenges of Friendship

As close as they were, Arya soon discovered that friendship, like family, came with its own set of challenges. While her bond with Leila brought her great happiness, it also tested her in ways she hadn't expected.

One day, while playing in the schoolyard, Arya overheard a group of children teasing Leila. Their words were sharp, cutting through the air like blades. They mocked Leila for being quiet, for keeping to herself, for not fitting in with the louder, more outgoing children in their class. Arya's heart clenched as she listened to their cruel words.

Without thinking, Arya stepped forward, ready to defend her friend. "Stop it!" she shouted, her voice trembling with anger. "Leave her alone!"

The children turned to Arya, surprised by her outburst. For a moment, there was silence. But then, as if emboldened by Arya's defiance, the teasing shifted. Now, it was directed at her.

"Look at Arya, always sticking up for Leila," one of the boys sneered. "Why don't you go sit with your weird friend, Arya? You're just as strange as she is!"

Arya felt the heat rise in her cheeks, a mixture of anger and embarrassment. She had expected to protect Leila, to be the hero in this moment. But now, she found herself on the receiving end of the same cruelty.

Leila, who had been silent during the exchange, gently touched Arya's arm. "It's okay," she whispered. "You don't have to fight for me."

Arya turned to her friend, confused. "But they were being mean to you," she said, her voice tight with frustration.

Leila smiled softly, her eyes filled with a quiet wisdom. "People say mean things sometimes," she said. "But their words don't define who I am. I know who I am, Arya, and that's enough."

Arya stared at her friend, the anger slowly melting away. Leila's words struck her deeply. She had always been quick to defend herself and others, to fight against injustice. But Leila's response was different—calm, centered, rooted in a sense of inner peace that Arya had never experienced.

In that moment, Arya realized that friendship wasn't just about standing up for each other—it was also about learning from each other. Leila had shown her a new way of being, a way of responding to the world that wasn't rooted in anger or defense, but in quiet strength and self-assurance.

The Soul's Recognition of Old Bonds

As the weeks passed, Arya and Leila's friendship deepened. They spent hours together, talking about everything from their favorite books to their dreams for the future. But as their connection grew, Arya couldn't shake the feeling that there was something more to their bond—something unspoken but profoundly familiar.

One afternoon, while they were lying on the grass beneath the large oak tree at school, Arya voiced the thought that had been lingering in her mind for weeks.

"Do you ever feel like we've met before?" Arya asked, her voice hesitant.

Leila turned her head to look at Arya, her eyes thoughtful. "What do you mean?"

Arya struggled to find the right words. "It's just... sometimes, I feel like we've known each other for a long time. Like we were friends before this life. Does that sound crazy?"

Leila was silent for a moment, her gaze distant as if she were searching for something deep within herself. Finally, she nodded. "No, it doesn't sound crazy," she said softly. "I've felt it too. It's like our souls recognize each other."

Arya felt a wave of relief wash over her. She hadn't been imagining it—Leila had felt the same connection, the same sense of familiarity.

"Maybe we were friends in another life," Arya mused, her voice filled with wonder.

Leila smiled, her expression serene. "Maybe we were."

For the first time, Arya began to consider the possibility that her relationships in this life were not new—they were continuations of connections formed long ago. The bond she shared with Leila was more than just a friendship—it was a thread that had woven its way through multiple lifetimes, a karmic connection that had brought them together once again to learn and grow.

The Lessons of Connection

As Arya's friendship with Leila continued to flourish, she began to understand the deeper lessons that came from human connection. Through her relationship with Leila, Arya learned about the importance of vulnerability, of being open to another person in a way that was both authentic and deeply honest.

Leila, with her quiet strength and inner peace, taught Arya the value of self-acceptance. She showed Arya that true confidence didn't come from external validation or approval—it came from knowing who you were, deep inside, and being at peace with that truth.

But Arya also learned that friendship, like all relationships, required patience and understanding. There were moments when she and Leila disagreed, when their differences created tension. But rather than allowing those moments to drive them apart, Arya and Leila used them as opportunities to grow—both as individuals and as friends.

In one such moment, Arya found herself feeling jealous of Leila. It was a small thing—Leila had been praised by their teacher for a drawing she had made, while Arya's own artwork had gone unnoticed. The jealousy surprised Arya, catching her off guard. She had never felt this way about Leila before, and the emotion made her feel ashamed.

Rather than keeping the feeling to herself, Arya decided to talk to Leila about it. One afternoon, as they sat together under the oak tree, Arya took a deep breath and confessed her feelings.

"I felt jealous of you today," Arya admitted, her voice quiet. "When Ms. Harper praised your drawing, I felt like... like I wasn't good enough. And I hated feeling that way, because you're my best friend. I didn't want to feel jealous of you."

Leila listened quietly, her expression thoughtful. When Arya finished speaking, Leila reached over and took her hand.

"It's okay to feel that way," Leila said softly. "I've felt jealous before too. It doesn't mean you don't love me. It just means you're human. We all feel that way sometimes."

Arya stared at her friend, her heart swelling with gratitude. Leila's response was full of grace and understanding, and in that moment, Arya realized that true friendship wasn't about being perfect—it was about being real. It was about sharing your vulnerabilities, your fears, and your insecurities, and trusting that the other person would hold space for them without judgment.

Through her friendship with Leila, Arya learned that connection was one of the most powerful forces in the world. It had the ability to heal wounds, to bridge divides, and to remind her of the deep, unspoken bond that connected all souls.

The Power of Human Connection

As Arya entered the later years of childhood, she began to form other friendships, each one teaching her something new about herself and the world. But no matter how many connections she made, her friendship with Leila remained special—a constant reminder of the power of human connection.

It was through these early relationships that Arya began to see the threads of karma weaving their way through her life. Each person she met, each friend she made, was part of the larger tapestry of her soul's journey. Some friendships would last a lifetime, while others would fade with time. But each one, no matter how brief, left an imprint on her soul.

Arya began to understand that human connection was one of the most profound aspects of life on Earth. It was through these connections that she would learn the most important lessons—lessons about love, forgiveness, compassion, and understanding. Each friendship, each relationship, was a reflection of her own soul, showing her the parts of herself that still needed to grow and evolve.

As Arya looked forward to the years ahead, she felt a deep sense of gratitude for the people in her life—for her family, for her friends, and for the connections that would continue to shape her journey. Life, she realized, was not just about the challenges she faced or the lessons she learned—it was about the people who walked beside her on that journey, helping her grow in ways she could never have imagined.

And as she gazed up at the sky, feeling the warmth of the sun on her face, Arya knew that her soul's journey was just beginning.

Chapter 13: Navigating Adolescence and Identity

The Struggles of Adolescence

As Arya transitioned into her teenage years, the world seemed to shift around her. The simplicity of childhood, once filled with the carefree days of friendship and play, began to give way to the more complex realities of adolescence. The changes in her body, her emotions, and her relationships felt overwhelming at times, as if the ground beneath her feet was constantly shifting.

For Arya, adolescence brought with it a growing sense of uncertainty. She no longer felt as sure of herself as she had in childhood. The confidence she had once had in her friendship with Leila and her sense of belonging in her family now seemed more fragile, more complicated.

At school, she found herself feeling increasingly out of place. While other girls her age were focused on boys, fashion, and fitting in, Arya often felt drawn to quieter, more introspective pursuits. She enjoyed spending time in nature, reading books about philosophy and spirituality, and reflecting on the deeper questions of life. But these interests often left her feeling isolated from her peers, who seemed more concerned with the latest trends and social dynamics.

"I just don't fit in," Arya confessed to Leila one afternoon as they sat together in the park. "Everyone else seems to know exactly who they are, what they want, and how to belong. But I feel like I'm always on the outside, like I don't belong anywhere."

Leila, ever the steady presence in Arya's life, smiled softly. "No one really knows who they are at this age, Arya. Everyone's just pretending. It's okay to feel lost sometimes. That's part of growing up."

Arya sighed, her heart heavy with the weight of uncertainty. She longed for the simplicity of childhood, when everything had felt so clear, so easy. But now, in the confusion of adolescence, she found herself questioning everything—her friendships, her identity, her place in the world.

The Question of Identity

As the months passed, Arya's struggle with identity deepened. She felt pulled in different directions, torn between the person she was and the person she thought she was supposed to be. At home, her parents had certain expectations for her—good grades, proper behavior, a clear path toward the future. At school, her peers seemed to expect something else entirely—popularity, conformity, the ability to fit neatly into the social landscape.

Arya found herself caught between these two worlds, unsure of where she truly belonged. She wanted to please her parents, to live up to their expectations, but she also craved acceptance from her peers. Yet, in trying to please everyone, she often felt as though she was losing herself in the process.

One evening, as Arya sat alone in her room, she stared at her reflection in the mirror. The face looking back at her seemed both familiar and foreign. Who was she, really? Was she the obedient daughter her parents wanted her to be? Was she the quiet, introspective girl who felt more comfortable in nature than at parties? Or was she something else entirely—someone she had yet to discover?

The question of identity weighed heavily on Arya's heart. She had always been sensitive to the expectations of others, but now, those expectations felt suffocating. She wanted to be true to herself, but she wasn't sure who that self was anymore.

"Who am I?" Arya whispered to the empty room, her voice filled with quiet desperation.

The answer didn't come right away. But deep within her, beneath the layers of confusion and doubt, Arya felt a small, steady presence—a quiet knowing that had always been there, waiting to be remembered. It was the voice of her soul, the part of her that remained untouched by the changing tides of adolescence.

"You are more than what others expect of you," the voice seemed to whisper. "You are more than the roles you play. You are a soul, a spark of the divine, and you are here to learn, to grow, to discover who you truly are."

The words brought Arya a small sense of peace, though the journey toward self-acceptance was far from over.

The Pressure to Conform

As Arya continued to navigate the complexities of adolescence, she felt the pressure to conform growing stronger. At school, the social dynamics seemed to revolve around fitting in—wearing the right clothes, saying the right things, and aligning with the right group of friends. Arya, who had always valued authenticity and individuality, found herself struggling to keep up with these unspoken rules.

One afternoon, as Arya and Leila walked through the halls of their school, they overheard a group of girls talking about an upcoming party. The excitement in their voices was palpable, and Arya felt a pang of longing. She wanted to be included, to be part of the group, but at the same time, she felt out of place in their world of social hierarchies and expectations.

"Are you going to the party?" one of the girls asked, turning to Arya with a raised eyebrow.

Arya hesitated, unsure of what to say. She had never been one for parties, preferring the quiet comfort of home or the peaceful solitude of nature. But in that moment, the pressure to fit in overwhelmed her.

"Maybe," Arya replied, her voice uncertain.

The girl smirked. "Well, if you do come, try not to wear anything too weird. You don't want to stand out too much."

The comment stung, and Arya felt her cheeks flush with embarrassment. She had never cared much about fashion, often opting for simple, comfortable clothes rather than the trendy outfits that seemed to dominate her school. But now, in the face of this subtle judgment, Arya felt the weight of her difference.

After the interaction, Leila turned to Arya, her expression sympathetic. "You don't have to go to the party, you know," she said gently. "You don't have to be like them."

Arya nodded, grateful for Leila's support, but the feeling of inadequacy lingered. She knew she didn't have to conform, but the pressure was still there, gnawing at her sense of self-worth.

For the first time, Arya began to realize that the greatest challenge of adolescence wasn't just about figuring out who she was—it was about learning how to stay true to that person in a world that often demanded conformity.

The Journey Toward Self-Acceptance

As Arya navigated the social pressures of adolescence, she began to confront the deeper issues of self-acceptance. The external world, with all its expectations and judgments, often left her feeling inadequate, as though she wasn't good enough just as she was. But as she grew older, Arya also began to understand that true self-worth couldn't be found in the approval of others—it had to come from within.

One evening, as Arya sat on her bed, flipping through an old journal, she came across an entry from when she was younger. It was a simple reflection, written in the early years of her childhood, when life had seemed much clearer.

"I like who I am," the entry read. "I like the way I think, the way I see the world. I don't want to change just to fit in."

Arya smiled sadly as she read the words. She had written them so confidently back then, before the pressures of adolescence had clouded her sense of self. But now, as she looked at the words with older eyes, she realized that the wisdom of her younger self was still true.

She didn't need to change to fit in. She didn't need to conform to anyone else's idea of who she should be. She was enough, just as she was.

In that moment, Arya made a quiet promise to herself—a promise to honor her own path, to embrace her uniqueness, and to stop trying to mold herself into someone she wasn't. The journey toward self-acceptance wouldn't be easy, and she knew there would be moments when the pressure to conform would feel overwhelming. But she also knew that her soul was guiding her, quietly reminding her of who she truly was.

"I am enough," Arya whispered to herself, her voice filled with quiet determination.

And for the first time in a long while, she believed it.

Embracing Authenticity

As Arya continued to grow, her journey toward self-acceptance became less about resisting external pressures and more about embracing her own authenticity. She realized that being true to herself wasn't just about rejecting conformity—it was about actively choosing to live in alignment with her values, her interests, and her inner truth.

One day, during a quiet moment at school, Arya found herself standing in front of the bulletin board, scanning the flyers for extracurricular activities. Most of them were for sports teams or clubs focused on popularity and socializing—things Arya had never been interested in. But then, a small flyer caught her eye: "Philosophy and Spirituality Club – A Space for Deep Thinkers and Seekers."

Arya's heart skipped a beat. She had always been drawn to questions of philosophy and spirituality, often finding solace in books and conversations that explored the deeper meaning of life. But she had never considered that there might be a space for people like her, a place where she could share her thoughts and ideas without feeling out of place.

Without hesitation, Arya pulled the flyer from the board and tucked it into her bag. She didn't know what to expect from the club, but something inside her told her that this was the kind of space she had been searching for—a space where she could be herself, without fear of judgment or exclusion.

That afternoon, Arya attended her first meeting of the Philosophy and Spirituality Club. The room was small, filled with a handful of students, each of them as quiet and thoughtful as Arya. The conversations were rich, filled with questions about the nature of existence, the meaning of life, and the journey of the soul.

For the first time in a long time, Arya felt at home. She didn't have to pretend to be someone she wasn't. She didn't have to fit into anyone else's expectations. Here, in this small, quiet room, Arya could simply be herself—a seeker, a thinker, a soul on a journey of discovery.

As the meeting ended and Arya walked home, a deep sense of peace settled over her. She realized that the path to authenticity wasn't about finding a place where she fit in—it was about creating her own place in the world, a place that aligned with who she truly was.

And in doing so, Arya was finally learning to embrace the most important lesson of all: that she was enough, just as she was.

Chapter 14: The Awakening of Purpose

A Restless Yearning

As Arya moved through her teenage years, the question of purpose began to stir more deeply within her. It was no longer enough to simply go through the motions of school, friendships, and family life. There was a growing sense of restlessness in her soul, a quiet but persistent yearning for something more.

It started as a whisper—small moments of dissatisfaction with the mundane routines of life. While her peers seemed content with the surface-level concerns of grades, popularity, and future careers, Arya found herself yearning for a deeper sense of meaning. She longed for a purpose that transcended the day-to-day, something that would connect her to the greater mysteries of existence.

"What am I really here for?" Arya often asked herself in the quiet moments of her day. It was a question that seemed to follow her everywhere, from the school hallways to the solitude of her bedroom. But despite her constant contemplation, the answer remained elusive.

One evening, while lying in bed, Arya stared up at the ceiling, her mind filled with thoughts of the future. The path ahead seemed both wide open and strangely undefined. She had no clear direction, no specific career aspirations like many of her classmates. All she knew was that there had to be more to life than what she saw on the surface.

"I want to do something that matters," Arya whispered to herself. "Something that helps people, that makes a difference."

The words hung in the air, filled with both hope and uncertainty. Arya didn't know what form her purpose would take, but she was certain of one thing: she was meant for something greater than the ordinary path.

Searching for Clarity

In her search for meaning, Arya began exploring new interests that aligned with her deeper sense of purpose. She devoured books on philosophy, spirituality, and the nature of existence, eager to uncover the wisdom of those who had walked the path before her. The questions that had once felt so overwhelming began to feel like opportunities for growth, like doors leading to new dimensions of understanding.

At school, Arya often found herself sitting quietly in class, her mind wandering to thoughts of the greater picture. While her classmates discussed test scores and college applications, Arya's thoughts were on a different track. She wondered about the nature of the soul, the purpose of life, and what it meant to live in alignment with one's higher self.

It was during one of these contemplative moments that Arya's philosophy teacher, Mr. Harper, noticed her quiet introspection.

"Lost in thought again, Arya?" he asked with a smile as the rest of the class worked on an assignment.

Arya glanced up, startled. She hadn't realized how deeply absorbed she had been in her own thoughts.

"Sorry, Mr. Harper," Arya replied softly. "I guess I'm just thinking about... everything."

Mr. Harper chuckled and pulled a chair over to sit beside her. "Everything is a lot to think about," he said gently. "What's on your mind?"

For a moment, Arya hesitated. She wasn't used to sharing her deeper thoughts with others, especially not with teachers. But something about Mr. Harper's calm presence made her feel safe, as if he truly wanted to understand.

"I've just been thinking about purpose," Arya said quietly. "About what we're really here for. It feels like everyone around me is so focused on school and grades and careers, but... I don't know. I just feel like there's more to life than that. I want to understand what my purpose is."

Mr. Harper nodded thoughtfully, his eyes filled with understanding. "That's a big question," he said. "And an important one. But it's also a question that can't always be answered right away. Sometimes, purpose reveals itself over time, as you move through life and experience different things. It's not something you can force—it's something you discover."

Arya considered his words carefully. She had been so focused on finding a clear answer, on defining her purpose in concrete terms. But maybe Mr. Harper was right—maybe her purpose wasn't something she could figure out all at once. Maybe it was something that would unfold gradually, as she lived her life and followed her passions.

Moments of Alignment

As Arya continued to reflect on her purpose, she began to notice small moments of alignment—times when her actions felt deeply connected to something greater than herself. These moments often came when she was helping others, whether it was tutoring a classmate, volunteering at a local shelter, or simply offering a listening ear to a friend in need.

There was something about these acts of service that filled Arya with a sense of peace and fulfillment. In those moments, the restlessness that had been gnawing at her soul seemed to fade away, replaced by a quiet knowing that she was exactly where she needed to be.

One afternoon, as Arya helped her mother prepare a meal for a neighborhood charity event, she felt a deep sense of gratitude wash over her. The work was simple—chopping vegetables, setting up tables—but there was something profoundly satisfying about contributing to a cause greater than herself.

As she chopped carrots in the kitchen, her mother looked over at her with a smile. "You've been really thoughtful lately, Arya," she said. "I've noticed you've been doing a lot of reading and reflecting. Is everything okay?"

Arya nodded, though she wasn't entirely sure how to explain the shift she had been feeling. "I've just been thinking a lot about what I want to do with my life," she said. "I want to make a difference, to help people. I just don't know how yet."

Her mother's smile deepened. "You don't have to have all the answers right now," she said gently. "You're still young, Arya. Your path will reveal itself in time. Just keep following what feels right to you."

As Arya listened to her mother's words, she felt a quiet sense of reassurance settle over her. Maybe she didn't need to know all the details of her purpose just yet. Maybe it was enough to follow the small moments of alignment, to trust that the path would unfold in its own time.

Trusting the Journey

As the months passed, Arya continued to search for ways to align her life with her deeper sense of purpose. She began volunteering more regularly at local shelters and community events, finding fulfillment in acts of service that connected her to others. Each time she gave of herself, she felt a little closer to understanding the true meaning of her existence.

But alongside these moments of fulfillment, Arya also faced moments of doubt. There were times when the path ahead seemed unclear, when the weight of uncertainty pressed down on her and made her question whether she would ever truly find her purpose.

During one particularly difficult week, when school assignments piled up and the demands of daily life felt overwhelming, Arya found herself sitting in the library, staring blankly at her notebook. The familiar restlessness had returned, and with it, a sense of frustration that she couldn't seem to shake.

"What if I never figure it out?" Arya whispered to herself, her voice tinged with worry. "What if I'm just wandering through life without any real direction?"

As she sat there, lost in her thoughts, she felt a gentle presence beside her. Leila had appeared, her quiet energy calming the storm of emotions swirling inside Arya.

"You look like you're carrying the weight of the world," Leila said softly as she sat down beside her.

Arya sighed, her shoulders slumping. "I just... I want to figure out what I'm supposed to do with my life," she said. "But every time I think I'm getting closer, I hit a wall. It feels like I'll never find my purpose."

Leila smiled, her eyes filled with understanding. "Arya, you're already living your purpose," she said gently. "It's not about some grand, distant goal that you'll reach one day. It's about the way you live your life every day. The way you care for people, the way you give of yourself, the way you show up in the world—that's your purpose. You're already doing it."

Arya blinked, surprised by the simplicity of Leila's words. Could it really be that simple? Had she been searching for something grand and elusive, when her purpose was already unfolding in the small moments of her daily life?

"You don't have to have it all figured out," Leila continued. "Just keep following what feels true to you. Trust that you're exactly where you're meant to be, even if it doesn't always make sense right now."

Arya felt a wave of relief wash over her. Leila's words, so simple yet profound, gave her permission to let go of the pressure to have all the answers. Maybe her purpose wasn't something she needed to search for—it was something she was already living, something that would continue to evolve as she followed her heart.

A New Sense of Purpose

As Arya left the library that afternoon, she felt lighter, as if a weight had been lifted from her shoulders. For the first time in a long time, she wasn't burdened by the need to define her purpose in concrete terms. Instead, she felt a quiet sense of trust in the journey, a knowing that her purpose would continue to unfold in its own time.

In the weeks that followed, Arya threw herself more fully into the activities that brought her joy and fulfillment. She continued to volunteer, to read, to reflect, and to seek out opportunities for growth and connection. With each passing day, she felt more aligned with her soul's mission, even if she couldn't yet see the full picture of where her path would lead.

The restlessness that had once plagued her began to fade, replaced by a deeper sense of peace and contentment. Arya realized that purpose wasn't about a singular goal or destination—it was about living each day with intention, with love, and with a commitment to making a positive impact in the world.

As she stood at the threshold of adulthood, Arya knew that her journey was far from over. There would be new challenges, new lessons, and new opportunities to grow. But she also knew that she was ready—ready to embrace whatever the future held, with the understanding that her purpose would continue to reveal itself as she followed the quiet whispers of her soul.

And in that knowing, Arya found the peace she had been searching for all along.

Chapter 15: The Turning Point

The Calm Before the Storm

Life, it seemed, had settled into a gentle rhythm for Arya. She had grown more comfortable with the idea that her purpose was not something she needed to rush toward but something that would unfold over time. Her days were filled with moments of alignment—volunteering, spending time with her friends, and nurturing the quiet parts of herself that had always been drawn to deeper meaning.

The restlessness that had once gnawed at her seemed to have quieted. For the first time in years, Arya felt a sense of peace, a contentment in simply being. She had learned to trust the journey, to let go of the need for certainty, and to embrace the mystery of her unfolding purpose.

But life, as Arya would soon discover, had its own plans. Just when she had begun to feel secure in her path, a sudden event would shake the very foundation of her world, forcing her to confront her deepest fears and testing her newfound sense of purpose in ways she had never imagined.

The Unexpected Loss

It happened on an ordinary afternoon, a day like any other. Arya had just returned home from school, her bag slung over her shoulder as she walked through the front door. Her mother greeted her with a soft smile, her hands busy preparing dinner in the kitchen. The scent of warm spices filled the air, and the house hummed with the quiet comfort of routine.

But the peace of that moment was shattered by the sudden ring of the phone. Arya's mother, wiping her hands on a towel, picked up the receiver. Arya noticed the shift in her mother's expression almost immediately. The smile that had graced her face just moments before vanished, replaced by a look of shock and disbelief.

"No..." her mother whispered, her voice trembling. "No, that can't be."

Arya stood frozen in the doorway, her heart pounding in her chest. She had never seen her mother look so pale, so fragile. Something was terribly wrong.

"What happened?" Arya asked, her voice barely audible.

Her mother didn't answer right away. She stood there, gripping the phone as though it were the only thing anchoring her to the world. Finally, after what felt like an eternity, she turned to Arya, her eyes filled with tears.

"It's your father," her mother said, her voice breaking. "There was an accident. He's... he's gone."

Gone.

The word echoed in Arya's mind, but it didn't make sense. How could her father be gone? He had just left for work that morning, like he did every day. He couldn't be gone. Not like this. Not so suddenly.

The room around her seemed to blur, and Arya felt a wave of disbelief crash over her. This couldn't be real. This couldn't be happening. But as the details of the accident were relayed over the phone, the truth slowly began to sink in.

Her father was gone. And nothing would ever be the same again.

The Weight of Grief

In the days that followed, Arya found herself enveloped in a fog of grief. The world around her seemed to move in slow motion, each day blurring into the next as she tried to process the enormity of the loss. Her father, who had always been a quiet, steady presence in her life, was gone, and the weight of his absence pressed down on her like a heavy stone.

The house, once filled with the comforting rhythms of daily life, now felt eerily quiet. Her mother moved through the days like a ghost, her eyes red from crying, her voice barely a whisper. And Arya, struggling to make sense of it all, found herself retreating into her own silence, unable to find the words to express the depth of her pain.

At school, everything felt different. The routine of classes and homework seemed trivial in the face of what had happened. Arya's friends tried to comfort her, but their words felt hollow, as if no one could truly understand the depth of her loss. Even Leila, who had always been a source of support, seemed distant in the face of Arya's grief.

One afternoon, as Arya sat alone in the library, staring blankly at the pages of a book she couldn't focus on, she felt a tear slip down her cheek. She hadn't cried much since the accident—her emotions felt too raw, too overwhelming. But in the quiet of the library, with no one around to witness her pain, the tears finally came.

"I don't understand," Arya whispered to herself. "Why did this happen? What's the point of it all?"

Her grief was not just for the loss of her father, but for the loss of the peace she had worked so hard to find. In the months before the accident, Arya had finally begun to feel a sense of purpose, a sense of alignment with her path. But now, that peace had been shattered, and she was left questioning everything.

Searching for Meaning in Loss

In the weeks that followed her father's death, Arya found herself grappling with questions that had no easy answers. The sense of purpose she had once felt so strongly now seemed distant, almost unreachable. How could she find meaning in a world where someone she loved could be taken from her so suddenly, so unfairly?

One evening, as Arya sat in her room, staring out the window at the darkening sky, she found herself thinking back to the conversations she had had with her guides before she was born—conversations that she could no longer fully remember but could still feel deep within her soul. She had chosen this life, chosen the challenges she would face. But had she really chosen this? This unbearable pain, this overwhelming sense of loss?

"Why would I choose this?" Arya whispered, her voice thick with emotion. "How could this be part of my path?"

The question echoed in her mind, but no answer came. Instead, there was only silence—the same silence that had followed her since the day her father had died.

For a long time, Arya sat there, staring out into the night, searching for some kind of clarity, some sense of meaning that could help her make sense of the loss. But the answers remained elusive.

It wasn't until much later, when Arya lay in bed, exhausted from the weight of her grief, that a quiet thought emerged from the depths of her soul.

"Maybe this is part of the journey," the thought whispered. "Maybe this pain, this loss, is here to teach you something you wouldn't have learned otherwise."

Arya didn't fully understand the thought, but something about it resonated with her. As much as she wanted to resist the idea that this loss could be part of her growth, she couldn't deny the quiet truth that was beginning to stir within her.

The Lesson of Resilience

As time passed, Arya slowly began to come to terms with her father's death. The grief didn't disappear—it was still there, lingering in the background of her days—but it began to take on a different shape. It became less of an overwhelming force and more of a quiet companion, something she carried with her but no longer let consume her.

In the weeks and months following the accident, Arya began to realize that grief, like all challenges, had its own lessons to teach. Through her loss, Arya had been forced to confront the fragility of life, the unpredictability of the human experience. But she had also learned about resilience—about the strength that comes from continuing on, even when everything inside you is telling you to give up.

One afternoon, as Arya sat beneath the oak tree in her backyard—the same tree where she had often sought solace as a child—she closed her eyes and let the quiet stillness of the moment wash over her. For the first time in a long while, she felt a sense of peace, not because the pain had disappeared, but because she had learned how to carry it.

"You're stronger than you think," Arya whispered to herself. "You can get through this."

In that moment, Arya understood that resilience wasn't about avoiding pain—it was about finding the strength to keep moving forward, even in the face of the greatest challenges. It was about allowing yourself to grieve, to feel the full weight of your emotions, and then choosing to rise again, stronger and more compassionate than before.

A Deeper Understanding of Purpose

As Arya moved through the aftermath of her father's death, she began to realize that her sense of purpose had not been lost—it had simply evolved. The meaning she had been searching for wasn't about avoiding pain or finding a clear, easy path through life. It was about embracing the full spectrum of human experience—the joys and the sorrows, the triumphs and the losses—and allowing each experience to shape her into the person she was meant to become.

In the months that followed, Arya continued to volunteer, to help others, and to seek out opportunities to make a difference in the world. But now, her actions were infused with a deeper sense of compassion, a quiet understanding that life was both beautiful and fragile, and that her purpose wasn't just about finding meaning for herself—it was about helping others find meaning in their own lives as well.

One afternoon, as Arya sat with her mother, helping her organize some old family photos, she looked at a picture of her father, his familiar smile frozen in time.

"I miss him," Arya said softly, her voice filled with both sadness and love.

Her mother nodded, her eyes brimming with tears. "I miss him too," she whispered. "Every day."

For a long moment, they sat in silence, the weight of their shared grief hanging in the air between them. But beneath the sadness, there was also a quiet sense of connection—a knowing that they were not alone in their pain, that they were walking this journey together.

And in that moment, Arya understood something she hadn't fully realized before: her purpose wasn't just about finding peace for herself—it was about helping others find peace too. It was about walking through the darkness with compassion and resilience, and helping others do the same.

Chapter 16: The Quiet Strength of Healing

Learning to Live with Grief

In the months following her father's death, Arya began to understand that healing wasn't a single moment or a sudden revelation. It was a slow, quiet process—one that required patience, self-compassion, and a willingness to let the pain coexist with moments of peace. Grief wasn't something to be "gotten over" or fixed—it was something she had to learn to live with.

At first, Arya resisted the idea. She wanted to move past the pain, to get back to the sense of purpose and contentment she had felt before her father's death. But as time went on, she realized that grief wasn't something she could leave behind. It had become a part of her, woven into the fabric of her life. And while it didn't define her, it had changed her in ways that she was only beginning to understand.

One evening, as Arya sat by the window, watching the sun set over the horizon, she thought about how much she had grown since the accident. The pain of losing her father had forced her to confront parts of herself she hadn't known existed—her resilience, her capacity for compassion, and her ability to find peace in the midst of suffering.

She had learned that healing wasn't about forgetting or moving on. It was about carrying the love and the pain together, allowing both to shape her in ways that made her stronger, more empathetic, and more deeply connected to the world around her.

The Support of Friendship

Throughout her healing process, Arya found that one of the most important sources of strength came from her friendships, particularly her bond with Leila. In the weeks following her father's death, Leila had been a constant presence in Arya's life, offering quiet support without ever pushing Arya to talk about her feelings before she was ready.

One afternoon, as they sat together on a bench in the park, Leila turned to Arya with a thoughtful expression.

"You've been so strong through all of this," Leila said softly. "I don't know how you do it."

Arya shrugged, her eyes downcast. "I don't feel strong," she admitted. "Most days, I just feel... tired. Like I'm just trying to get through the day."

Leila nodded, her expression understanding. "That's okay. Healing isn't easy. But you're doing it, even if it doesn't always feel that way."

Arya glanced up at her friend, grateful for her quiet support. Leila had been there for her in ways that no one else had—offering her presence, her understanding, and her friendship without expecting anything in return. It was through this friendship that Arya began to understand the true meaning of support—not just being there in the good times, but standing by someone's side during their darkest moments.

"I don't think I could have gotten through this without you," Arya said, her voice filled with gratitude.

Leila smiled, her eyes soft. "You would have," she said gently. "But I'm glad I could be here with you."

In that moment, Arya realized how much she had leaned on Leila during her grief, and how much her friendship had been a lifeline through the storm of emotions she had faced. Leila had shown her that healing didn't have to be a solitary journey. Sometimes, the strength to heal came from the love and support of those who cared for you.

The Power of Helping Others

As Arya continued to navigate her own healing, she found herself drawn more and more toward helping others who were going through their own struggles. There was something about being of service, about offering a listening ear or a kind word, that brought her a sense of purpose and peace.

One afternoon, as Arya volunteered at a local shelter, she met a young woman named Sarah who was struggling with the recent loss of her mother. As they sat together in the quiet corner of the shelter, Sarah began to open up about her grief, her voice trembling with the weight of the emotions she had been carrying.

"I don't know how to keep going," Sarah admitted, her eyes filled with tears. "It just feels so heavy. Like it's never going to get better."

Arya listened quietly, her heart aching for Sarah. She remembered all too well the suffocating weight of grief, the way it seemed to cloud every moment of life, making it hard to imagine a future beyond the pain.

"I know it feels like that now," Arya said gently. "And I won't tell you that the pain will ever completely go away. But it will get easier to carry. With time, you'll find ways to hold the grief and the love together, and you'll learn how to live again."

Sarah wiped at her tears, her expression filled with both sorrow and a flicker of hope. "How do you know that?" she asked softly.

Arya smiled, a quiet strength radiating from within her. "Because I've been there," she said simply. "And I'm still learning how to live with it too."

As they sat together, Arya felt a deep sense of connection to Sarah, a bond that went beyond their shared experience of loss. It was through these moments—through helping others navigate their own pain—that Arya began to see the deeper meaning of her own journey. Her grief had given her the capacity to understand, to empathize, and to offer support in ways she hadn't been able to before.

Rediscovering Her Purpose

As Arya continued to heal, she found that her sense of purpose had taken on new dimensions. The desire to help others, which had always been a part of her, now felt more urgent, more meaningful. She realized that her own healing wasn't just for herself—it was for the people she could help along the way, for the connections she could make, and for the impact she could have on the world.

Through volunteering, through small acts of kindness, and through her quiet moments of reflection, Arya began to feel her purpose unfolding more clearly. It wasn't about grand gestures or world-changing accomplishments—it was about being present, about showing up for others with compassion, and about living in alignment with the values that mattered most to her.

One evening, as Arya sat with her mother in the living room, the soft glow of the lamp casting warm shadows across the walls, her mother turned to her with a gentle smile.

"I've been thinking a lot about your father lately," her mother said, her voice soft. "About how much he cared for people. He didn't always show it in big ways, but he had such a quiet way of helping others. I see that same spirit in you."

Arya felt a lump rise in her throat, her heart swelling with emotion. She had spent so much of her life trying to understand her purpose, trying to find her place in the world. And now, hearing her mother's words, she realized that her father's quiet strength and compassion had been passed down to her in ways she hadn't fully recognized.

"Thank you," Arya said softly, her voice filled with gratitude. "I hope I can live up to that."

Her mother smiled, her eyes brimming with love. "You already are."

The Strength of Compassion

As Arya reflected on her journey, she realized that compassion had been the common thread that had carried her through both her own healing and her interactions with others. It was compassion that had allowed her to forgive herself for the moments when she felt lost or overwhelmed. It was compassion that had helped her navigate her grief and offer comfort to those who were suffering.

And it was compassion that had become the foundation of her purpose—the quiet, steady force that guided her in everything she did.

One afternoon, as Arya walked through the park, the sun warm on her face, she felt a deep sense of peace settle over her. She had learned that healing wasn't about erasing the pain—it was about learning to carry it with grace. It was about allowing the wounds to shape her into a stronger, more compassionate person, and using that strength to help others on their own journeys.

As she sat down on a bench, watching the world around her, Arya closed her eyes and took a deep breath. In that moment, she felt the quiet strength of healing—the knowledge that she had come through the storm and was still standing, still moving forward, still living with purpose.

And in that quiet moment, Arya knew that her journey was far from over. There would be more challenges, more lessons, and more opportunities to grow. But she also knew that she had the strength, the resilience, and the compassion to face whatever came next.

Because healing, she had learned, wasn't a destination—it was a journey. And it was a journey that she was ready to embrace, one step at a time.

Chapter 17: A New Beginning

The Transition to Adulthood

As Arya approached her eighteenth birthday, she found herself standing on the edge of a new chapter in her life. Adulthood loomed ahead, filled with both uncertainty and possibility. The girl who had once struggled with questions of identity and purpose now felt a deeper sense of who she was, even if there were still many unanswered questions about the future.

The transition into adulthood felt both exciting and overwhelming. Arya had graduated from high school with honors, and now, the world seemed to stretch out before her, filled with choices she wasn't sure how to make. College, careers, and relationships all seemed to demand her attention, pulling her in different directions.

"You're growing up," her mother said one evening as they sat at the dinner table. "I'm so proud of the woman you're becoming."

Arya smiled at the words, but beneath her calm exterior, there was a quiet anxiety building. She knew that everyone around her expected her to have a plan—to know what she wanted to do, where she wanted to go, and how she would build her future. But Arya still felt uncertain. She wasn't ready to commit to a single path, and the pressure to make decisions weighed heavily on her.

"Do I really have to have it all figured out right now?" Arya asked one afternoon as she sat with Leila in their favorite spot at the park.

Leila laughed softly, shaking her head. "Of course not," she said. "No one really has it all figured out. Life is about exploring, discovering, and letting things unfold in their own time."

Arya sighed, feeling a sense of relief at her friend's words. She had been so focused on the expectations of adulthood—on making the "right" choices—that she had forgotten that life was a journey, not a destination. Maybe it was okay not to have all the answers right away.

The Power of Choice

As Arya prepared to leave home and step into the next phase of her life, she realized that the choices she made now would shape the course of her future. But rather than feeling trapped by the weight of those choices, Arya began to see them as opportunities—opportunities to create a life that aligned with her values, her passions, and her soul's purpose.

One afternoon, as Arya sat in her room, surrounded by college brochures and application forms, she felt a quiet moment of clarity settle over her. She didn't have to follow the same path as everyone else. She didn't have to choose a career or a future based on what others expected of her. She could make choices that felt right for her, even if they didn't follow the traditional path.

With this realization, Arya decided to take a gap year before starting college. She wanted time to explore, to travel, and to discover more about herself and the world before committing to a specific direction. It wasn't the choice that her friends or family had expected, but it felt right for Arya.

When she told her mother about her decision, she braced herself for resistance. But to her surprise, her mother smiled and nodded.

"I think that's a wonderful idea," her mother said. "You've always been someone who follows her own path. I'm proud of you for making this choice."

Arya felt a wave of gratitude wash over her. The decision to take a gap year wasn't about escaping responsibility—it was about giving herself the time and space to grow, to reflect, and to align her life with the deeper purpose that had been calling to her for so long.

The Journey Begins

With her gap year decided, Arya set out to make plans for her time away from school. She wanted to travel, to volunteer, and to immerse herself in new experiences that would broaden her understanding of the world. But more than that, she wanted to use this time to deepen her connection to her soul's purpose.

In the weeks leading up to her departure, Arya felt a mixture of excitement and nervousness. She had never been away from home for an extended period, and the thought of traveling to unfamiliar places felt both thrilling and daunting. But beneath the uncertainty, there was a quiet confidence building within her—a sense that this was the right step, even if she didn't know exactly where it would lead.

"You're really going to do it, aren't you?" Leila said one evening as they sat together, discussing Arya's plans.

Arya nodded, a small smile playing at the corners of her lips. "Yeah, I am," she said. "It feels like the right time."

Leila grinned, her eyes filled with admiration. "I'm proud of you," she said. "You've always been brave, Arya. You've never been afraid to follow your heart."

As they sat in the fading light of the evening, Arya felt a deep sense of gratitude for her friendship with Leila. Their bond had carried her through some of the most challenging moments of her life, and now, as she prepared to step into a new chapter, Arya knew that Leila's support would continue to be a source of strength.

"You'll keep in touch, right?" Leila asked, her voice filled with quiet concern.

"Of course," Arya replied, reaching out to squeeze her friend's hand. "We'll always be connected, no matter where I am."

A World of Possibilities

As the day of her departure approached, Arya packed her bags and prepared for the journey ahead. She had chosen to start her travels in a small village in Southeast Asia, where she would volunteer at a community center that provided education and resources to underprivileged children. The work aligned perfectly with Arya's passion for helping others, and she was eager to immerse herself in the experience.

On the morning of her flight, Arya stood at the airport with her mother, Leila, and a few close friends. The air was filled with a mix of emotions—excitement, nervousness, and a sense of the unknown.

"You're going to do amazing things," her mother said, pulling her into a tight hug. "I'm so proud of you for following your heart."

Arya smiled, her eyes brimming with emotion. "Thank you, Mom," she whispered. "I'll miss you."

As Arya turned to say goodbye to Leila, the two friends embraced, holding onto each other for a moment longer than usual.

"I'm going to miss you," Leila said softly. "But I know this is exactly what you need to do."

Arya nodded, her heart full. "I'll miss you too," she replied. "But this isn't goodbye. It's just the beginning."

With one final wave to her friends and family, Arya turned and walked toward the gate, her heart pounding with a mixture of excitement and anticipation. She didn't know what the future held, but she knew that this was her path—one that would lead her to new experiences, new challenges, and new opportunities for growth.

As the plane took off, lifting her into the sky, Arya felt a sense of freedom unlike anything she had ever experienced before. The world stretched out before her, vast and full of possibilities, and Arya was ready to embrace it all.

Finding Purpose in the Unexpected

When Arya arrived at the village where she would be volunteering, she was immediately struck by the simplicity and beauty of the place. The community was close-knit, the people warm and welcoming. The work was challenging, but it was also deeply fulfilling. Each day, Arya spent time with the children, teaching them basic reading and writing skills, playing games, and helping with day-to-day tasks at the community center.

But more than the work itself, it was the connections Arya formed that left the deepest impact on her. The children, with their bright smiles and eager hearts, reminded Arya of the power of human connection—the same connection she had felt with Leila and with the people she had helped back home.

One afternoon, as Arya sat with a group of children, helping them with their lessons, a young girl named Mei tugged at her sleeve.

"Why did you come here?" Mei asked, her dark eyes filled with curiosity. "You could be anywhere in the world. Why did you come to our village?"

Arya paused, considering the question. In truth, she had come here searching for something—clarity, purpose, a deeper understanding of herself. But now, as she sat with Mei and the other children, she realized that the answer was much simpler.

"I came here because I wanted to help," Arya said softly. "But I think I'm the one who's learning the most."

Mei smiled, her expression thoughtful. "You're helping a lot," she said quietly. "We're glad you're here."

As Arya looked around at the faces of the children, she felt a deep sense of fulfillment settle over her. She had always believed that her purpose was to help others, but now, in this small village on the other side of the world, Arya was beginning to understand that her purpose was something she lived every day—through the connections she made, the kindness she offered, and the love she shared.

Embracing the Journey

As Arya's gap year unfolded, she continued to grow, both as a person and as a soul on a journey of discovery. The work she did in the village, the relationships she built, and the challenges she faced all contributed to a deeper understanding of her place in the world.

But more than anything, Arya had learned to embrace the journey itself. She had let go of the need to have all the answers, the need to define her purpose in concrete terms. Instead, she had found peace in the knowledge that her purpose was something that would continue to evolve as she moved through life.

One evening, as Arya stood on a hill overlooking the village, the sun setting in the distance, she took a deep breath and smiled. She had come here searching for clarity, but what she had found was far more profound.

She had found herself.

And as Arya looked out at the world before her, she knew that this was only the beginning.

Chapter 18: The Call to Serve

The Rewards of Service

As the weeks passed in the village, Arya found herself growing more deeply connected to the people around her. The children, once shy and reserved, now greeted her with wide smiles and open arms each day. The elders of the village, with their quiet wisdom and warm presence, welcomed her into their homes, sharing stories of their lives, their challenges, and their dreams for the future.

For Arya, these connections were more than just fleeting moments of kindness—they were windows into a deeper understanding of what it meant to serve others. She had come to the village thinking that she would be the one giving, the one helping, but she quickly realized that she was receiving just as much, if not more, from the people she served.

There was a simple beauty in the daily routines of the village—in the shared meals, the laughter of the children, and the sense of community that permeated every interaction. Arya felt a deep sense of fulfillment in being part of something larger than herself, in contributing to a cause that was rooted in love and care for others.

But alongside the rewards of service came new challenges—challenges that would test Arya's resilience and her commitment to living a life of purpose.

The Challenge of Exhaustion

As fulfilling as her work was, Arya soon discovered that dedicating herself fully to service was not without its costs. The days were long, and the work was physically and emotionally demanding. There were times when she felt utterly exhausted, her body aching from the constant movement, her mind weary from the endless demands.

One evening, after a particularly exhausting day at the community center, Arya collapsed onto her bed, her muscles sore and her mind heavy with the weight of the day's events. She had spent hours helping the children with their lessons, and then worked late into the evening preparing food and organizing supplies for the center.

Despite her exhaustion, Arya felt a sense of satisfaction in knowing that she had made a difference. But she also knew that she couldn't continue like this forever. The constant giving, without taking time for herself, was beginning to wear her down.

As Arya lay in the darkness, staring up at the ceiling, she wondered how she could find a balance between serving others and taking care of herself. She wanted to give her all to the people she had come to love, but she also knew that she couldn't pour from an empty cup.

The lesson, Arya realized, was not just about serving others—it was about learning how to sustain that service over the long term. And that meant taking care of herself, too.

Learning to Find Balance

In the weeks that followed, Arya began to make small changes to her routine, carving out moments of rest and reflection in the midst of her busy days. She started waking up early to meditate by the river, allowing herself time to center her mind and reconnect with the quiet voice of her soul. She also began to set boundaries around her work, learning to say no when she felt overwhelmed and to ask for help when she needed it.

It wasn't easy at first. Arya had always been someone who wanted to give her all, to push herself to the limit in the name of helping others. But slowly, she began to realize that taking care of herself wasn't selfish—it was necessary. If she wanted to continue serving others in a meaningful way, she had to ensure that her own well-being was a priority, too.

One afternoon, as Arya sat by the river, watching the sunlight dance on the water's surface, she felt a sense of peace settle over her. The river, with its steady flow and gentle current, reminded her of the importance of balance. Just as the river needed both movement and stillness, so too did Arya need both action and rest.

In that moment, Arya made a silent promise to herself: she would continue to give, to serve, and to help others. But she would also honor her own needs, ensuring that she had the strength and energy to sustain her work over the long term.

The Unexpected Challenge

As Arya continued her work in the village, she encountered an unexpected challenge—one that would test not only her resilience but also her sense of purpose. One afternoon, as Arya was helping the children with their lessons, the head of the community center, Mr. Liu, approached her with a serious expression.

"Arya," he said quietly, "we've received word that the funding for the center is being cut. We'll have to make some difficult decisions in the coming weeks."

Arya felt her heart sink. The community center was the heart of the village—the place where children came to learn, where families received support, and where the community gathered to share in the joys and challenges of daily life. Without it, the village would lose a vital resource.

"What can we do?" Arya asked, her voice filled with concern.

Mr. Liu sighed, his expression weary. "We're exploring our options," he said. "But the truth is, without the funding, we may have to scale back our services or close the center altogether."

Arya felt a wave of frustration rise within her. She had come to the village to make a difference, to help build something lasting and meaningful. But now, it seemed as though all of her efforts, and the efforts of the people she had come to care for, were in jeopardy.

For the first time since she had arrived, Arya felt powerless. The challenges she had faced before—exhaustion, homesickness, uncertainty—seemed small in comparison to this. How could she continue to serve when the very foundation of her work was at risk of crumbling?

A Call for Action

Despite her initial feelings of helplessness, Arya knew that she couldn't simply stand by and watch as the community center's future hung in the balance. She had come here to help, and she wasn't about to give up without a fight.

In the days that followed, Arya threw herself into action. She worked with Mr. Liu and the other volunteers to organize fundraising efforts, reaching out to donors and sponsors who might be willing to support the center. She also rallied the village, encouraging the community to come together and advocate for the importance of the center's work.

It wasn't easy. There were moments when Arya felt as though they were fighting an uphill battle—when the donations didn't come in as quickly as they had hoped, or when the challenges seemed too great to overcome. But through it all, Arya held onto the belief that their work mattered, that their efforts were worth fighting for.

One evening, as Arya sat with Mr. Liu in the quiet of the empty community center, she felt a wave of exhaustion wash over her. They had been working tirelessly for weeks, and while they had made progress, the future of the center was still uncertain.

"Do you think it will be enough?" Arya asked, her voice filled with quiet worry.

Mr. Liu smiled, his expression gentle. "I don't know," he admitted. "But what I do know is that we're doing everything we can. And sometimes, that has to be enough."

Arya nodded, feeling a sense of quiet determination settle over her. She had come to the village with a desire to serve, to make a difference. And while the road ahead was uncertain, Arya knew that she was on the right path—one that was filled with both challenges and rewards, but one that was deeply aligned with her soul's purpose.

A Victory for the Village

After weeks of tireless effort, the day finally came when Arya and the other volunteers would learn the fate of the community center. As they gathered in the small office, waiting for news from the donors, Arya felt her heart pounding in her chest. She had poured everything she had into this effort—her time, her energy, her heart—and now, the future of the center hung in the balance.

When the phone rang, Mr. Liu answered with a calm expression, though Arya could see the tension in his eyes. As he listened to the voice on the other end of the line, his expression slowly shifted, a small smile tugging at the corners of his lips.

"Thank you," he said, his voice filled with quiet relief. "Thank you so much."

As he hung up the phone, he turned to the room, his smile widening. "We did it," he said softly. "The funding has been secured. The center will stay open."

A wave of cheers and applause erupted in the room, and Arya felt tears prick at the corners of her eyes. It had been a long, difficult journey, filled with moments of doubt and uncertainty. But in the end, their efforts had paid off. The community center—the heart of the village—would continue to serve the people who needed it most.

As the celebrations continued around her, Arya stood in the quiet of the office, feeling a deep sense of fulfillment settle over her. This was why she had come here—to help, to serve, and to make a difference. And now, as she looked around at the faces of the people she had come to love, Arya knew that she had found her place.

Embracing the Call

In the weeks that followed, Arya continued her work at the community center, but now, there was a new sense of purpose guiding her. The experience of fighting to keep the center open had shown her the power of perseverance, the strength of community, and the importance of standing up for what you believe in.

More than that, it had deepened her commitment to a life of service. Arya knew that there would be more challenges ahead—both for herself and for the people she served. But she also knew that she had the strength, the resilience, and the heart to face those challenges head-on.

As Arya stood at the riverbank one afternoon, watching the water flow steadily toward the horizon, she felt a quiet sense of peace. She had chosen this path—a path of service, of compassion, of making a difference in the lives of others. And now, she was ready to embrace it fully.

Whatever the future held, Arya knew that she was exactly where she was meant to be.

Chapter 19: Returning Home

The End of the Journey Abroad

As Arya's gap year drew to a close, she found herself standing on the hill overlooking the village, the place that had become a second home to her. The months she had spent there had been filled with both challenges and triumphs, and as she prepared to return to her life back home, Arya couldn't help but feel a mixture of emotions.

There was excitement in the thought of reuniting with her family and friends, of returning to the familiar routines and comforts of home. But there was also a quiet sadness, a sense of loss that came with leaving behind the people and the place that had become such a central part of her journey.

As Arya packed her bags for the trip home, she reflected on how much she had changed during her time abroad. The girl who had arrived in the village months ago—uncertain of her path, unsure of her place in the world—now felt stronger, more confident, and more deeply connected to her purpose.

"You've made such a difference here," Mr. Liu said one evening as they sat together by the river, the gentle sound of the water filling the air. "The community is stronger because of you. You've left a lasting impact."

Arya smiled, her heart full. "I've learned so much from everyone here," she replied. "It feels like this place has given me more than I could ever give back."

Mr. Liu nodded, his eyes filled with warmth. "That's the beauty of service," he said. "It's not about what you give or what you get—it's about the connections you make, the lives you touch, and the way those connections change you."

As Arya sat by the river that evening, she realized that while her journey in the village was coming to an end, the lessons she had learned and the connections she had made would stay with her for the rest of her life.

Reconnecting with Home

When Arya stepped off the plane and into the familiar embrace of her mother and Leila, she felt a rush of emotions. The sight of her mother's warm smile, the familiar scent of home, and the sound of her friend's laughter filled her with a sense of comfort and belonging.

But as Arya settled back into her life at home, she couldn't shake the feeling that something had shifted. The world she had once known so well now felt different, almost distant, as if she were seeing it through new eyes. The experiences she had lived through abroad—the challenges, the connections, the growth—had changed her in ways that were difficult to put into words.

One afternoon, as Arya and Leila sat together in the park, Leila turned to her with a curious expression.

"You seem different," Leila said softly. "Not in a bad way—just... more confident. Like you know something the rest of us don't."

Arya smiled, a quiet laugh escaping her. "I don't know about that," she said. "But I do feel different. The time I spent away—it changed me. I've learned so much about myself, about what I want, about what really matters."

Leila nodded, her eyes thoughtful. "I can see that," she said. "You've always been someone who follows her heart, but now... it feels like you've found something deeper, like you've really figured out who you are."

Arya paused, considering Leila's words. In many ways, she had found a deeper understanding of herself during her time abroad. The journey had given her clarity, not only about her purpose but also about the strength that came from trusting her own path, even when it led her into the unknown.

"I think I've learned to trust myself more," Arya said quietly. "I've realized that I don't have to have all the answers right away. It's okay to just be in the moment, to let things unfold as they're meant to."

A New Perspective on Life

As the weeks passed, Arya found herself re-entering the routines of daily life—spending time with her family, catching up with old friends, and making plans for the future. But beneath the surface of these familiar activities, Arya carried with her a new perspective—one that had been shaped by her time abroad and by the people she had met along the way.

Her mother noticed the change in Arya almost immediately. One evening, as they sat together in the living room, her mother turned to her with a gentle smile.

"You seem so much more at peace now," her mother said. "It's like the restlessness that used to follow you around has disappeared."

Arya smiled, her heart warmed by her mother's observation. "I think it has," she admitted. "I used to feel like I needed to figure everything out, like I was always searching for something. But now, I feel more settled. I've realized that the journey is the answer, that it's okay to not have everything planned out."

Her mother nodded, her expression filled with pride. "I'm so proud of you, Arya," she said softly. "You've grown into such a strong, thoughtful woman. I can see how much your time away has changed you."

As they sat together, Arya felt a deep sense of gratitude for the support of her family. It had been their encouragement, their belief in her, that had given her the courage to take the leap and embark on her gap year. And now, as she prepared to move forward with the next phase of her life, Arya knew that she carried their love and support with her, no matter where her journey led.

Returning to Service

As Arya settled back into life at home, she felt a renewed sense of purpose guiding her. While she had returned from her travels with a deeper understanding of herself, she also knew that her commitment to service remained at the core of her purpose.

One day, as Arya sat in her room reflecting on her time in the village, she felt a familiar pull—one that called her to continue her work of helping others. The lessons she had learned abroad, the connections she had made, had shown her the power of community, the importance of compassion, and the impact that even small acts of kindness could have on the world.

Inspired by her experiences, Arya began exploring ways to bring the spirit of service back to her own community. She started volunteering at a local organization that provided support to underserved families, using the skills and knowledge she had gained during her gap year to help those in need.

As Arya worked with the families in her community, she felt the same sense of fulfillment that she had experienced in the village abroad. The faces were different, the challenges unique, but the core of the work remained the same: offering compassion, understanding, and support to those who needed it most.

And in those moments of service, Arya knew that she was living her purpose—not because she had all the answers or had figured out her future, but because she was showing up each day with an open heart, ready to give and to grow.

A New Chapter Begins

As Arya continued her work in the community, she felt a deep sense of contentment settle over her. She had come a long way from the girl who had once felt lost and uncertain, searching for meaning in a world that seemed too big to navigate. Now, Arya understood that her purpose wasn't something she needed to find—it was something she lived every day through her actions, her connections, and her commitment to making the world a better place.

One evening, as Arya sat with Leila in their favorite spot at the park, Leila turned to her with a smile.

"So, what's next for you?" Leila asked, her voice filled with curiosity. "You've been through so much, and now that you're back, what do you want to do?"

Arya paused, looking out at the horizon as the sun began to set. The future stretched out before her, filled with possibilities she couldn't yet see. But for the first time in her life, Arya didn't feel the pressure to have it all figured out. She didn't need a plan, a roadmap, or a clear destination.

"I'm not sure yet," Arya replied, her voice calm and steady. "But I know that whatever comes next, I'm ready for it. I'm ready to keep learning, to keep growing, and to keep following my heart."

Leila smiled, her eyes filled with admiration. "I think that's the best plan of all."

As they sat together, watching the sun dip below the horizon, Arya felt a deep sense of peace. She had learned that life wasn't about finding a single purpose or reaching a final destination—it was about embracing the journey, with all its twists and turns, and trusting that each step would lead her closer to the person she was meant to become.

And with that quiet knowing, Arya welcomed the next chapter of her life with open arms.

Chapter 20: The Path of Compassion

A New Role in the Community

After settling back into life at home, Arya's commitment to service became the cornerstone of her daily existence. Her experiences abroad had opened her heart and mind to the endless possibilities of human connection, and she now found herself stepping into a leadership role at the local organization where she volunteered.

The organization, dedicated to helping underserved families, was in need of someone to oversee the day-to-day operations, and Arya's passion for service, combined with her experience abroad, made her the perfect fit. Though she hadn't initially sought a leadership role, Arya felt a deep sense of responsibility to use what she had learned to help strengthen the community.

"You're exactly what we need," said Ms. Thompson, the director of the organization, during their first meeting. "Your experience and dedication to helping others have inspired everyone here. I believe you can really make a difference."

Arya nodded, her heart swelling with both excitement and a touch of nervousness. Leading the organization meant more than just helping with tasks—it meant creating opportunities for growth, for healing, and for positive change within the community.

"Thank you," Arya replied softly. "I'll do my best."

And with that, Arya embraced her new role, determined to bring the same compassion and resilience she had cultivated abroad into her work at home.

Building a Community of Healing

As Arya began her work with the organization, she quickly realized that the needs of the community were vast. Families struggled with everything from food insecurity to housing issues to emotional trauma, and it was clear that the resources the organization provided—while crucial—were only a small piece of what was needed.

But Arya, with her growing sense of purpose, wasn't deterred. She knew that healing was a process, one that required not just practical solutions but also emotional and spiritual support. And so, in addition to overseeing the logistics of the organization's programs, Arya set out to create a space where people could feel seen, heard, and supported on a deeper level.

One of her first initiatives was to start a weekly gathering, where members of the community could come together to share their stories, their struggles, and their hopes for the future. Arya believed that true healing began with connection—with the ability to be vulnerable in a safe space and to know that others were walking alongside you on the journey.

The gatherings were small at first—just a handful of people sitting in a circle, sharing their experiences. But over time, word spread, and more and more people began to attend, drawn by the sense of community that Arya had fostered.

One evening, after the group had finished their discussion, an older woman named Mrs. Patel approached Arya with tears in her eyes.

"Thank you for creating this space," Mrs. Patel said quietly. "I've been carrying so much pain for so long, and I didn't realize how much I needed to be heard until now."

Arya smiled, her heart full. "You're not alone," she said gently. "We're all here for each other."

In that moment, Arya realized that her role as a leader wasn't just about organizing programs or providing services—it was about building a community of healing, where people could find strength in their shared humanity.

The Challenge of Compassion Fatigue

As the weeks went by, Arya poured herself into her work with the organization, dedicating long hours to the families she served and ensuring that the community had access to the resources they needed. But as fulfilling as the work was, Arya also began to feel the weight of the emotional toll it took on her.

The stories she heard—the struggles, the heartache, the pain—began to settle in her heart, making it harder and harder to maintain the sense of balance she had worked so hard to cultivate. While Arya had learned how to take care of herself abroad, she now found herself slipping back into old patterns of giving too much, without taking enough time to rest and recharge.

One evening, as Arya sat alone in her apartment, exhausted from a particularly challenging day, she felt a wave of doubt wash over her. Could she really continue on this path? Could she keep giving, day after day, without burning out?

"I'm so tired," Arya whispered to herself, her voice heavy with emotion. "I want to help, but I don't know if I can keep going like this."

The exhaustion she felt wasn't just physical—it was emotional, a kind of compassion fatigue that had crept up on her without her realizing it. Arya had always been someone who wanted to help others, to ease their burdens, but now she found herself carrying those burdens in ways that left her feeling drained.

It was a lesson she had learned before, but one she was now being forced to relearn: in order to help others, she had to take care of herself first.

The Importance of Boundaries

In the days that followed, Arya began to reflect on the importance of boundaries—both in her work and in her personal life. She had always believed that true service required giving all of yourself, but now she realized that in order to serve sustainably, she needed to set limits on how much she could give at any one time.

With this new awareness, Arya began to make changes to her routine. She started taking regular breaks during the day, making time for meditation and quiet reflection in the mornings, and allowing herself to say no when she felt overwhelmed. She also began reaching out to others for support, relying on her team at the organization to share the workload and trusting them to carry the mission forward with her.

One afternoon, as Arya sat with Ms. Thompson to discuss the direction of the organization, she opened up about her struggle with compassion fatigue.

"I've been feeling so exhausted," Arya admitted. "I love this work, but I'm realizing that I need to find a way to balance my own needs with the needs of the community."

Ms. Thompson nodded, her expression filled with understanding. "You're not alone in that, Arya," she said gently. "It's something we all face in this line of work. But it's important to remember that you can't pour from an empty cup. Taking care of yourself isn't selfish—it's necessary."

Arya felt a sense of relief wash over her. She had always admired Ms. Thompson's wisdom and experience, and hearing her speak so openly about the challenges of service made Arya feel less alone in her own struggle.

"Thank you," Arya said softly. "I think I needed to hear that."

Ms. Thompson smiled, her eyes filled with warmth. "We're in this together," she said. "And together, we'll figure out how to keep moving forward."

The Power of Compassion for Self

As Arya continued to navigate the balance between service and self-care, she began to realize that compassion wasn't just something she needed to extend to others—it was something she needed to give to herself as well. In order to truly live a life of purpose, Arya knew she had to honor her own needs, to treat herself with the same kindness and understanding that she offered to the people around her.

One evening, after a particularly long day, Arya took a walk by the river, the cool evening air refreshing against her skin. As she walked, she thought about all that she had learned over the past year—about service, about healing, and about the importance of staying true to herself.

She had always believed that compassion was her calling, her purpose in life. But now, Arya understood that in order to live that purpose fully, she had to start with herself. She had to be gentle with her own heart, to allow herself moments of rest and reflection, and to remember that even in her desire to help others, she was deserving of the same care and kindness.

As she stood by the river, watching the water flow steadily toward the horizon, Arya felt a deep sense of peace settle over her. She didn't have to have all the answers, and she didn't have to carry the weight of the world on her shoulders. What mattered most was that she showed up each day with an open heart, ready to give and ready to receive.

And in that quiet moment, Arya made a promise to herself: she would continue to walk the path of compassion, not just for others, but for herself as well.

Chapter 21: The Ripple Effect of Kindness

Inspiring Change

As Arya continued her work at the organization, she began to notice a subtle but powerful shift within the community. The gatherings she had initiated, once small and intimate, had grown into something much larger—an essential part of the fabric of the community's life. People from all walks of life came together to share their stories, their struggles, and their dreams, and in the process, they discovered the strength that came from connection and support.

But more than that, Arya noticed that the kindness and compassion she had cultivated within herself were beginning to spread. The people she had helped—those who had once been weighed down by their own challenges—were now helping others. They were paying it forward, offering the same kindness and understanding that they had received, and in doing so, they were creating a ripple effect of compassion that extended far beyond the walls of the organization.

One afternoon, as Arya sat in a circle with a group of community members, a young woman named Sofia spoke up.

"I've been coming to these gatherings for a few months now," Sofia said, her voice filled with emotion. "And I just wanted to say thank you. These meetings have changed my life. They've given me hope, and they've shown me that I'm not alone."

Arya smiled, her heart swelling with gratitude. "You've been such an important part of this community, Sofia," she said gently. "Your courage and your openness have helped so many people here. You've inspired all of us."

Sofia blushed, her eyes glistening with tears. "I never thought I'd be in a position to help anyone," she admitted. "But being here, with all of you, has shown me that even the smallest act of kindness can make a difference. And I want to keep doing that—I want to keep helping others, just like you've helped me."

As Arya listened to Sofia's words, she felt a deep sense of fulfillment settle over her. This was what it was all about—creating a space where people could heal, where they could find strength in each other, and where they could pass that strength on to others. The ripple effect of kindness was real, and Arya was watching it unfold before her eyes.

The Growth of the Organization

As the ripple effect of kindness spread through the community, the organization itself began to grow in ways Arya hadn't anticipated. More and more people were coming forward, eager to contribute their time, their skills, and their resources to the work Arya and her team were doing. What had once been a small, struggling nonprofit was now becoming a thriving hub of support and empowerment for the entire community.

Ms. Thompson, who had overseen the organization for many years, approached Arya one day with a thoughtful expression.

"You've done incredible things here, Arya," Ms. Thompson said, her voice filled with admiration. "The organization has grown so much under your leadership, and it's clear that your passion for helping others has inspired everyone around you."

Arya blushed, feeling both proud and humbled by Ms. Thompson's words. "Thank you," she said softly. "But I couldn't have done any of this without the support of everyone here. It's been a team effort."

Ms. Thompson nodded, her smile widening. "That's true," she said. "But every team needs a leader—someone with a vision, someone who can bring people together. And you've been that leader, Arya. You've shown us what's possible when we lead with compassion."

Arya felt a lump rise in her throat. The work she had done with the organization had never been about personal recognition—it had always been about helping others, about creating a space where people could find hope and healing. But hearing Ms. Thompson's words made Arya realize that her leadership had made a difference, not just in the lives of the people she served, but in the organization itself.

"You've built something truly special here," Ms. Thompson continued. "And I believe that this is only the beginning. There's so much more we can do—so many more people we can help."

Arya nodded, her heart swelling with a sense of possibility. She had always believed that small acts of kindness could create big change, but now she was seeing that change in action. The organization had become a beacon of hope for the community, and Arya was ready to keep pushing forward, to keep expanding their reach and impact.

A Community of Leaders

One of the most beautiful outcomes of Arya's work was the way in which it empowered others to step into their own roles as leaders. The people who had once come to the organization seeking help were now leading their own initiatives, creating new programs and support systems that extended far beyond what Arya had originally envisioned.

One evening, as Arya sat in the office, reviewing plans for an upcoming community event, a young man named Jaden knocked on the door.

"Hey, Arya," Jaden said with a grin. "Do you have a minute? I wanted to talk to you about something."

Arya smiled and gestured for him to come in. "Of course, Jaden. What's on your mind?"

Jaden had been one of the organization's most active volunteers for several months, and Arya had always admired his enthusiasm and dedication. But today, there was something different in his expression—something excited, almost nervous.

"I've been thinking," Jaden began, his voice filled with energy. "There's a group of teens in the neighborhood who could really use some guidance. A lot of them are struggling in school, and they don't have anyone to help them with their homework or just talk to them about life. I was thinking maybe we could start a mentoring program—something where volunteers like me can work with them one-on-one, give them the support they need."

Arya's eyes lit up. "Jaden, that's an amazing idea," she said, her voice filled with admiration. "We've needed something like that for a long time. I think you're the perfect person to lead it."

Jaden blushed, clearly surprised by Arya's confidence in him. "You really think I could do it?" he asked, his voice tinged with uncertainty.

"I know you can," Arya replied firmly. "You've already made such a difference here, Jaden. This mentoring program could change so many lives, and I think you're exactly the right person to make it happen."

Jaden's face broke into a wide grin, and Arya could see the excitement in his eyes. "I'll do it," he said, his voice filled with determination. "I'll start planning it right away."

As Jaden left the office, Arya felt a deep sense of pride and fulfillment. The ripple effect of kindness wasn't just about the people she had helped directly—it was about the leaders she had inspired, the people who were now stepping up to create their own impact.

And in that moment, Arya realized that her work had gone far beyond what she had ever imagined. She wasn't just helping others—she was empowering them to help themselves, to lead, and to create positive change in their own lives and the lives of those around them.

The Legacy of Compassion

As Arya reflected on all that had been accomplished in the past year, she felt a deep sense of gratitude for the journey she had been on. What had started as a simple desire to serve had blossomed into something much larger—a movement of compassion that was changing lives, one act of kindness at a time.

The organization had grown, the community had strengthened, and the people Arya had worked with had become leaders in their own right. But more than that, Arya had discovered the true power of compassion—the way it could heal, uplift, and transform not just individuals, but entire communities.

One afternoon, as Arya stood by the river, watching the water flow steadily by, she thought about the legacy she was leaving behind. It wasn't about recognition or accolades—it was about the lives she had touched, the people she had inspired, and the ripple effect of kindness that would continue to spread long after she was gone.

In that quiet moment, Arya felt a deep sense of peace. She had followed her heart, trusted her path, and lived her purpose. And in doing so, she had created something beautiful—something that would continue to grow and thrive, touching countless lives in ways she couldn't even begin to imagine.

As Arya stood there, bathed in the soft light of the afternoon sun, she knew that her journey was far from over. There were still new challenges to face, new lessons to learn, and new opportunities to make a difference. But she was ready for whatever came next.

Because Arya had learned that true purpose wasn't about the destination—it was about the journey. And it was a journey she was honored to continue walking, with compassion as her guide.

Chapter 22: Challenges of Leadership

The Weight of Responsibility

As the organization continued to grow, Arya found herself stepping into a new phase of leadership—one that came with both exciting opportunities and unexpected challenges. The community had embraced the programs she and her team had developed, and the impact of their work was evident in the lives they touched. But with that success came the weight of responsibility, and Arya began to feel the pressure of managing not just the day-to-day operations but also the long-term vision for the future.

At first, Arya welcomed the responsibility. She was proud of what they had accomplished, and she was excited about the possibilities for expanding their reach. But as the demands of leadership grew, so did the pressure. There were more decisions to make, more people relying on her, and more expectations to meet. The balance she had worked so hard to maintain between her personal well-being and her work began to slip, and Arya found herself once again struggling to find time for rest.

One evening, as Arya sat alone in her office, reviewing a proposal for a new program, she felt the familiar pang of exhaustion settle over her. The day had been filled with back-to-back meetings, and there were still emails to answer, budgets to review, and plans to finalize. Despite the satisfaction that came with the success of the organization, Arya couldn't shake the feeling that she was running on empty.

"I don't know how much longer I can keep this up," Arya whispered to herself, her voice tinged with frustration. "There's always so much to do, and never enough time."

As she leaned back in her chair, Arya realized that she was once again falling into the same pattern she had struggled with before—pushing herself too hard, giving too much, without taking the time she needed to recharge. It was a lesson she had learned before, but one that she now had to learn again in the context of leadership.

Seeking Support

The next morning, Arya woke up feeling the weight of the previous day still pressing on her. She knew that something needed to change, but she wasn't sure how to lighten the load without compromising the work they were doing. After all, the success of the organization had always been her top priority.

As she sipped her coffee and thought about the challenges she faced, Arya decided to reach out to Ms. Thompson, her mentor and the former director of the organization. Ms. Thompson had always been a source of wisdom and guidance, and Arya knew that she could offer valuable insight into how to navigate the complexities of leadership.

When they met later that afternoon, Ms. Thompson greeted Arya with a warm smile, but her eyes immediately picked up on the exhaustion written across Arya's face.

"You've been working yourself too hard again, haven't you?" Ms. Thompson said gently, her tone filled with understanding.

Arya sighed, nodding. "I don't know how to avoid it," she admitted. "There's just so much to do, and I feel like everyone is counting on me. I don't want to let anyone down."

Ms. Thompson nodded thoughtfully. "I understand," she said. "Leadership comes with a lot of responsibility, and it's easy to feel like you have to carry it all on your own. But Arya, you're not alone in this. You have a team—a group of people who care just as much as you do about the work you're doing. You don't have to do it all by yourself."

Arya frowned, her mind racing with thoughts of all the tasks that still needed to be done. "But how do I let go?" she asked. "How do I trust others to take on more when I feel like I need to be in control of everything?"

Ms. Thompson smiled gently. "Trust is the key," she said. "You've built something amazing here, and part of being a good leader is knowing when to step back and let others step up. You've empowered your team to lead in their own ways—now it's time to trust them to do it."

As Arya listened to Ms. Thompson's words, she felt a wave of relief wash over her. She had always prided herself on being hands-on, on being involved in every aspect of the organization's work. But now, Arya realized that true leadership wasn't about doing everything herself—it was about empowering others to take on responsibility and trusting them to succeed.

Learning to Delegate

In the days that followed, Arya began to take Ms. Thompson's advice to heart. She started by having honest conversations with her team, explaining that she needed their help in managing the growing demands of the organization. At first, it was difficult for Arya to let go of control, but she soon realized that her team was more than capable of handling the tasks she had been holding onto.

One of her first steps was delegating the management of the new mentoring program to Jaden, the young man who had originally proposed the idea. Arya had always been involved in every aspect of the program's development, but now she decided to step back and let Jaden take the lead.

"Are you sure you're ready to trust me with this?" Jaden asked, a mix of excitement and nervousness in his voice.

Arya smiled, placing a hand on his shoulder. "I believe in you, Jaden," she said. "You've already done so much for this program, and I know you're going to take it even further. I'm here if you need guidance, but this is your project now."

Jaden beamed with pride, and Arya felt a sense of satisfaction in knowing that she had made the right decision. In the weeks that followed, Jaden took the program to new heights, expanding its reach and bringing in more volunteers to mentor the teens in the community. His leadership allowed Arya to focus on other areas of the organization, and she saw firsthand how empowering others could create even greater impact.

As Arya continued to delegate responsibilities, she noticed a shift within herself. The pressure she had once felt to do everything was slowly lifting, replaced by a sense of trust in her team. The organization was thriving, not because of Arya's individual efforts, but because of the collective strength of the people she had empowered to lead.

Balancing Leadership and Self-Care

With more of the day-to-day responsibilities delegated to her team, Arya began to find more time to focus on her own well-being. She made a conscious effort to return to the self-care practices that had once brought her peace—morning meditation, quiet walks by the river, and time spent journaling her thoughts and reflections.

At first, it felt strange to take time for herself in the midst of such a busy schedule. But as Arya reconnected with the practices that nourished her soul, she began to realize just how important those moments of stillness were. They gave her the clarity and energy she needed to lead with compassion and purpose, and they reminded her that she didn't have to sacrifice her own well-being in order to make a difference.

One evening, as Arya sat by the river, watching the sun set over the horizon, she felt a deep sense of peace settle over her. The challenges of leadership were still there, but they no longer felt overwhelming. She had learned to trust her team, to delegate responsibility, and to create space for herself to recharge.

In that quiet moment, Arya reflected on how far she had come—how the girl who had once struggled to find her purpose had now become a leader in her community, inspiring others to make a difference and empowering them to lead in their own ways.

But more than that, Arya realized that true leadership wasn't about doing it all—it was about finding balance, trusting in the strength of others, and leading with both compassion and humility.

The Wisdom of Letting Go

As Arya continued to navigate the complexities of leadership, she found that one of the greatest lessons she had learned was the wisdom of letting go. It wasn't about relinquishing responsibility or stepping away from the work that mattered—it was about trusting others to carry the vision forward, knowing that the impact of their collective efforts would be far greater than anything she could achieve alone.

The ripple effect of kindness that Arya had set in motion was no longer something she had to manage or control—it had taken on a life of its own, spreading through the community in ways she could never have anticipated. The people she had once served were now serving others, and the organization she had helped grow was thriving because of the passion and dedication of the team she had empowered.

One afternoon, as Arya met with her team to discuss future plans for the organization, she felt a deep sense of pride in the work they had done together. The challenges they had faced, the lessons they had learned, and the lives they had touched were all a testament to the power of compassion, collaboration, and trust.

"We've built something incredible here," Arya said, her voice filled with gratitude. "And it's because of all of you—your dedication, your hard work, and your belief in what we're doing."

Her team smiled, their faces reflecting the same sense of pride and fulfillment that Arya felt. Together, they had created something lasting—something that would continue to grow and evolve long after Arya's individual leadership role had ended.

As the meeting ended and Arya looked around at the people she had come to respect and admire, she knew that she was exactly where she was meant to be. She had learned to lead with love, to trust in the strength of others, and to embrace the challenges of leadership with an open heart.

And in that knowledge, Arya found the peace she had been searching for all along.

Chapter 23: The Circle of Life

A Season of Change

As the seasons shifted from summer to autumn, Arya noticed a quiet shift within herself as well. The pace of her life, once filled with the excitement of new projects and expanding responsibilities, had begun to slow. The organization was thriving, her team was strong, and the community was flourishing. Yet, Arya felt a subtle restlessness—a sense that change was on the horizon, though she wasn't sure what form it would take.

It was a quiet Saturday morning when Arya first began to sense that something was shifting. She sat on her porch, wrapped in a blanket, watching the leaves fall gently from the trees. The air was crisp, filled with the smell of rain and earth, and Arya found herself lost in thought, reflecting on the journey she had been on.

She had accomplished so much over the past few years—her work with the organization had brought her deep fulfillment, and the connections she had made with the people in her community had filled her heart. But as she watched the changing landscape of the world around her, Arya began to wonder if it was time for her to embrace a new chapter in her life.

A Family Milestone

It wasn't long after Arya began to feel this inner restlessness that a significant event occurred in her family. Her younger sister, Rhea, who had been living abroad for the past few years, announced that she was engaged to be married and was planning to return home for the wedding.

The news brought joy to Arya's heart, and she looked forward to reconnecting with Rhea after so much time apart. The wedding preparations filled their family home with excitement and anticipation, and Arya found herself swept up in the flurry of activity—helping Rhea plan the ceremony, selecting flowers, and attending dress fittings.

But amid the celebration, Arya also felt a sense of nostalgia and reflection. Watching her sister prepare for this new chapter in her life reminded Arya of the many transitions she herself had been through—the moments of growth, the lessons learned, and the changes that had shaped her into the person she had become.

One afternoon, as Arya and Rhea sat together in their childhood home, reminiscing about their past, Rhea turned to Arya with a thoughtful expression.

"You've been through so much, Arya," Rhea said softly. "You've built an incredible life for yourself. But I can't help but wonder... what's next for you?"

Arya smiled, her eyes distant as she thought about Rhea's question. "I'm not sure yet," she admitted. "I've been feeling like something is changing inside me, like I'm ready for the next step, but I don't know what that is yet."

Rhea nodded, her eyes filled with understanding. "It sounds like you're in the same place I was a few years ago—on the edge of something new, but not quite sure what it is. Maybe this wedding will give you the clarity you need."

Arya laughed softly. "Maybe," she said. "Or maybe I just need to give myself the time to figure it out."

Letting Go of the Familiar

As the wedding approached, Arya found herself reflecting more and more on the idea of letting go—of allowing old chapters to close so that new ones could begin. Her work with the organization had been fulfilling in ways she could never have imagined, but she wondered if it was time for her to step back and allow others to take the lead.

The idea of letting go wasn't an easy one. Arya had poured her heart and soul into the organization, and it had become a central part of her identity. But as she watched her sister prepare for her new life, Arya began to realize that change was a natural part of growth, and that sometimes, stepping aside was the most compassionate choice she could make for herself and for those around her.

One evening, as Arya sat with Ms. Thompson in the quiet office of the organization, she voiced the thoughts that had been weighing on her heart.

"I've been thinking about stepping back," Arya said quietly. "The team is strong, and the community is thriving. I feel like it might be time for me to move on, to make space for new leadership."

Ms. Thompson studied Arya for a moment, her eyes filled with both understanding and curiosity. "What's making you feel this way?" she asked gently.

Arya took a deep breath, searching for the right words. "I think it's just... time," she said. "I've loved this work, but I'm feeling called to something else—something I haven't quite figured out yet. I don't want to hold onto this role out of fear of letting go. I want to make space for whatever comes next."

Ms. Thompson smiled, her expression soft. "You've always had a good sense of when it's time to move forward," she said. "It takes courage to recognize when a chapter is closing and to trust that the next one will reveal itself in time."

As they sat together in the quiet of the office, Arya felt a sense of peace settle over her. She didn't know exactly what the future held, but she knew that it was time to trust the flow of life and to allow herself the freedom to explore new possibilities.

The Wedding and the Next Step

The day of Rhea's wedding arrived with all the joy and beauty that Arya had hoped for. The ceremony was held in a sunlit garden, surrounded by family and friends, and as Rhea walked down the aisle, Arya felt a surge of emotion. Her sister had grown into a confident, radiant woman, ready to embrace the next phase of her life with love and hope.

As Arya stood by Rhea's side during the vows, she couldn't help but think about her own journey—about the changes she had gone through, the lessons she had learned, and the new beginnings that awaited her. Watching Rhea take this significant step made Arya even more certain that her own life was about to shift in ways she couldn't yet predict.

After the ceremony, as Arya and Rhea shared a quiet moment together, Rhea turned to Arya with a smile.

"Are you ready for whatever comes next?" Rhea asked, her voice filled with affection.

Arya laughed softly, nodding. "I think so," she said. "It's time for a new chapter, for both of us."

Embracing the Unknown

In the weeks that followed the wedding, Arya officially stepped down from her role as director of the organization, passing the leadership to Jaden and the rest of the team. It wasn't an easy decision, but Arya knew in her heart that it was the right one. She had built something beautiful, and now it was time to trust others to carry it forward.

With her days no longer filled with meetings and planning, Arya found herself with a sense of freedom she hadn't felt in years. At first, the quiet was unsettling—after so long in a leadership role, she wasn't used to having so much time for herself. But as the days went by, Arya began to embrace the stillness, using it as an opportunity to reflect on what truly mattered to her.

She spent her mornings by the river, journaling and meditating, and her afternoons exploring new hobbies—painting, writing, and volunteering in smaller, quieter ways. The restlessness she had once felt began to dissolve, replaced by a deep sense of peace and acceptance.

As Arya looked out at the world, she realized that the circle of life was always turning—new beginnings, new endings, and the constant flow of change. It was a cycle she had once resisted, but now, Arya welcomed it with open arms.

She didn't know exactly what her next chapter would look like, but for the first time in her life, Arya was okay with not knowing. She trusted that life would continue to guide her, just as it always had, and that each step she took would lead her exactly where she was meant to be.

Chapter 24: The Journey Inward

A Time for Reflection

As the months passed and Arya settled into her new rhythm, she found herself drawn more deeply inward. With the daily demands of running the organization behind her, Arya had more time than ever to reflect on her life, her choices, and the deeper purpose that had always guided her. It was a time of stillness, of quiet contemplation, and of seeking answers to the questions that had lingered in her heart for so long.

Without the constant need to plan or manage, Arya's days unfolded with a sense of ease she hadn't experienced in years. She spent her mornings in meditation, allowing herself to connect with the quiet voice of her soul, and her afternoons exploring the natural world around her. The river, the forest, and the open sky became her companions during this time of reflection, reminding her of the beauty and simplicity of life.

But even in the stillness, Arya knew that this period of reflection was not an end in itself—it was a preparation for something more. She could feel a subtle pull toward deeper spiritual exploration, toward uncovering the parts of herself she hadn't yet fully understood. The questions she had once asked about her purpose and her place in the world had evolved, becoming less about external actions and more about inner alignment.

One evening, as Arya sat by the river watching the stars, she felt a quiet knowing settle over her—a sense that this time in her life was about more than just rest. It was about transformation.

The Call to Spiritual Growth

Arya had always felt a connection to the spiritual side of life, but it wasn't until this period of reflection that she truly began to explore it more deeply. She found herself drawn to books and teachings about the soul, about the nature of existence, and about the journey of the spirit beyond the physical world.

Through her readings, Arya discovered new perspectives on life and purpose—ideas that resonated with her in a way that felt both familiar and profound. The teachings she encountered spoke of the soul's eternal nature, of the lessons we come to Earth to learn, and of the connections we form with others across lifetimes. These ideas echoed the thoughts Arya had long carried with her, the sense that her life was part of a much larger tapestry of experiences and growth.

One afternoon, while reading a passage about the soul's journey, Arya felt a deep sense of recognition wash over her. The words spoke of how each lifetime was chosen by the soul to learn specific lessons, to heal old wounds, and to evolve in love and understanding. It was a concept Arya had always believed in, but now, with this newfound clarity, it took on an even deeper significance.

"We choose our lives," Arya whispered to herself, her voice filled with quiet awe. "We choose our challenges, our joys, our experiences—all of it, for the growth of our soul."

This realization filled Arya with a sense of peace. For so long, she had been searching for meaning in the external world, in her actions and accomplishments. But now, Arya understood that the true journey was an inward one, and that the lessons she had come to learn were as much about her inner growth as they were about her external impact on the world.

Embracing Solitude

As Arya continued to deepen her spiritual practice, she began to embrace solitude in a way she never had before. What had once felt like loneliness now felt like a gift—a sacred space in which she could listen to the whispers of her soul without distraction.

In this quiet space, Arya allowed herself to let go of the need for constant productivity. She spent her days in meditation, in prayer, and in quiet contemplation, allowing herself to simply be. It was a radical shift from the life she had once led—filled with meetings, responsibilities, and the constant pressure to help others. Now, Arya realized that helping others was only one part of her purpose. The other part was to help herself—to heal, to grow, and to deepen her connection to the divine.

One morning, as Arya sat by the river in meditation, she felt a sense of expansion within her—a feeling that went beyond her physical body, beyond her mind, and beyond the limitations of time and space. It was as if her soul had stretched out, touching the infinite, and in that moment, Arya understood that she was part of something much larger than herself.

The realization brought tears to her eyes, not out of sadness, but out of a deep, overwhelming sense of love. Love for the world, love for the people she had met along her journey, and love for the soul that she was—a soul that had chosen this life, with all its challenges and joys, for the purpose of growth and evolution.

In that moment, Arya felt more connected to herself, and to the divine, than she ever had before.

The Inner Journey as Purpose

As Arya moved further into her journey of self-discovery, she began to understand that her purpose had always been twofold: to serve others and to serve herself. The work she had done in the community had been a vital part of her path, but so too was this time of introspection, this deep exploration of her soul's journey.

It was during this time that Arya came to a profound realization: the outward journey and the inward journey were not separate—they were deeply interconnected. Her work in the world had been a reflection of her inner growth, and now, her inner work would continue to shape the way she moved through the world.

In one of her meditations, Arya received a clear message from within—a message that spoke to the balance she had been seeking all along.

"You are here to grow," the voice whispered gently. "In every action, in every choice, you are learning. Your purpose is not in the outcome, but in the experience. Trust the process, and trust that you are exactly where you are meant to be."

The words filled Arya with a sense of peace she had never known before. She had always believed in her purpose, but now she understood it on a deeper level. Her life was not about achieving a specific goal or reaching a certain milestone—it was about the ongoing process of becoming, of evolving, of learning to love and be loved.

This realization shifted Arya's perspective on everything. She no longer felt the need to push herself toward external achievements or to measure her worth by the impact she made on others. Instead, she focused on the inner work—on aligning her actions with the love and compassion she felt in her heart.

Returning to the World

As Arya's time of deep reflection continued, she began to feel a quiet pull to re-engage with the world around her. The months she had spent in solitude had been transformative, but Arya knew that the lessons she had learned weren't meant to stay hidden within her. They were meant to be shared, to be expressed through her actions, and to be lived in the world.

One afternoon, as Arya walked through the forest near her home, she felt the familiar sense of clarity that always came when she was connected to nature. She realized that her journey wasn't about choosing between the inward and outward paths—it was about integrating both.

The time she had spent in solitude had given her the tools she needed to live with greater purpose and intention. She now understood that her work in the world didn't have to be separate from her inner journey. In fact, the two were inseparable. The more she aligned with her soul's purpose, the more naturally her actions would reflect that alignment.

With this understanding, Arya made a quiet decision: she would return to the community she had helped build, not as a leader trying to control the outcome, but as a participant in the shared journey of growth and healing. She would continue to serve, not from a place of obligation or pressure, but from a place of love and connection.

Arya knew that the journey inward had prepared her for this next phase of her life. She was ready to return to the world, not as the person she had been before, but as someone who had learned to trust herself, her soul, and the divine flow of life.

A New Beginning

As Arya prepared to re-engage with the world, she felt a deep sense of gratitude for the time she had spent in solitude. It had been a period of profound growth, of healing, and of reconnecting with her soul's purpose. And now, as she stepped into the next chapter of her life, Arya felt ready—ready to embrace the challenges and opportunities that lay ahead, with a heart full of love and a spirit grounded in peace.

The river, which had been her constant companion during this time of reflection, flowed steadily beside her, a reminder that life was always moving, always changing. And as Arya stood by the water's edge, watching the current carry the leaves downstream, she smiled, knowing that she, too, was part of that flow.

Her journey wasn't over—it was just beginning.

Chapter 25: The Cycle of Returning

Coming Home

Arya's return to the community felt both familiar and new. The streets, the people, and the rhythms of daily life had remained unchanged in many ways, yet Arya felt different—more grounded, more present, and more connected to the deeper truths she had uncovered during her time of solitude. She was stepping back into a world she knew well, but with a renewed sense of clarity and purpose.

When Arya walked through the doors of the community center, the place that had once been her second home, she was greeted with warm smiles and open arms. Jaden, now fully established as the organization's leader, welcomed her back with a grin that reflected both respect and gratitude.

"You've been missed," Jaden said, giving Arya a warm hug. "The work you started here has grown in ways you wouldn't believe."

Arya smiled, her heart swelling with pride for the team she had once led. "I'm so proud of everything you've done," she replied. "I never doubted that you and the team would carry the vision forward."

Jaden's eyes sparkled with excitement as he led Arya through the center, showing her the new programs and initiatives that had been launched during her time away. The mentoring program had expanded, new volunteers had joined the team, and the community's engagement had deepened. It was clear that the seeds Arya had planted had blossomed into something even more impactful than she could have imagined.

As Arya walked through the bustling center, watching the volunteers and community members working together in harmony, she felt a deep sense of peace. She no longer needed to be at the helm—her role had evolved, and she was now here to offer guidance, support, and the wisdom she had gained from her own journey.

Sharing the Wisdom of the Journey

One of the most meaningful aspects of Arya's return was the opportunity to share the insights and wisdom she had gained during her time of solitude. People in the community, especially those she had mentored in the past, began seeking her out for advice, not just on practical matters but on the deeper questions of life—purpose, healing, and the journey of the soul.

One afternoon, as Arya sat in the garden behind the community center, a young woman named Maya approached her with a quiet, thoughtful expression.

"Arya, can I talk to you for a moment?" Maya asked, her voice filled with uncertainty.

Arya smiled warmly and gestured for Maya to sit beside her. "Of course," Arya said. "What's on your mind?"

Maya hesitated for a moment before speaking. "I've been feeling... lost lately," she admitted, her eyes downcast. "I'm not sure what I'm supposed to be doing with my life. I've been trying to figure out my purpose, but nothing seems clear. I thought you might have some advice."

Arya nodded, understanding the depth of Maya's struggle. She had been in that place of uncertainty herself, many times over the years. But now, with the clarity she had gained from her own journey, Arya knew that the answers Maya was seeking wouldn't come from anyone else—they would come from within.

"I know how hard it can be to feel lost," Arya said gently. "But sometimes, the feeling of being lost is exactly what leads us to where we need to be. It's a signal that we're ready to grow, to go deeper, and to discover new parts of ourselves."

Maya looked up, her eyes filled with curiosity. "But how do I find my purpose?" she asked. "How do I know what I'm meant to do?"

Arya smiled softly. "Your purpose isn't something you have to find," she explained. "It's something that unfolds as you live, as you follow what feels true to you in each moment. The more you connect with yourself—with your heart, your intuition, your soul—the more your path will reveal itself."

Maya considered Arya's words, a look of quiet understanding dawning on her face. "So it's not about having all the answers right away," she said slowly. "It's about trusting the process."

"Exactly," Arya said, her voice filled with warmth. "Your purpose isn't a destination—it's a journey. And every step you take, every experience you have, is part of that journey. Trust yourself, and trust that you are exactly where you're meant to be."

As Maya nodded, a sense of peace seemed to settle over her. Arya could see that the young woman had begun to understand the deeper truth she had been searching for—that purpose wasn't something to be forced or figured out, but something that emerged naturally through living in alignment with one's true self.

Leading Through Presence

As Arya continued to re-engage with the community, she found that her role had shifted in subtle but profound ways. She was no longer focused on managing or directing the organization—instead, she had become a source of quiet wisdom, offering guidance through presence rather than control. People came to her not for instructions but for insight, for the deeper understanding that could only come from someone who had walked their own path of transformation.

One afternoon, as Arya sat with Jaden and the leadership team discussing the future of the organization, Jaden turned to her with a question.

"You've been through so much, Arya," Jaden said thoughtfully. "How do you stay grounded? How do you keep going, even when things get overwhelming?"

Arya smiled, her eyes soft with understanding. "I've learned that it's not about avoiding challenges or trying to control everything," she said. "It's about staying present with what is—whether it's joy or struggle, success or failure—and trusting that every experience is part of the journey. The more I've learned to let go of the need for control, the more I've found peace in simply being present."

Jaden nodded, his expression thoughtful. "I guess that's easier said than done," he admitted. "I still feel like I need to have all the answers, to make sure everything runs smoothly."

Arya chuckled softly. "It's a process," she said. "But remember—you don't have to have all the answers. No one does. Leadership isn't about knowing everything—it's about being open, being willing to learn, and trusting the people around you to contribute their strengths."

As Jaden absorbed Arya's words, she could see the quiet shift in his perspective. The weight of leadership, which had once felt so heavy for both of them, was beginning to lighten, replaced by a deeper understanding of what it meant to lead with presence, trust, and humility.

The Power of Surrender

Throughout her time back in the community, Arya continued to deepen her practice of surrender—the art of letting go and allowing life to unfold without forcing outcomes. It was a lesson she had learned during her time of solitude, but now, in the context of her relationships and her work, Arya realized just how powerful surrender could be.

One evening, as Arya sat by the river reflecting on her journey, she thought about the times in her life when she had felt the most lost—when she had struggled to find her place in the world, to understand her purpose, or to make sense of the challenges she had faced. In each of those moments, it had been surrender—letting go of the need to control or fix—that had brought her back to herself.

"Surrender isn't about giving up," Arya whispered to herself. "It's about trusting that life has a rhythm, a flow, and that when we align with that flow, everything falls into place."

As Arya sat by the river, watching the water flow steadily by, she felt a deep sense of peace settle over her. She no longer needed to chase after purpose or success. She no longer needed to prove her worth through accomplishments. She had learned to trust the process, to trust herself, and to trust that the journey would continue to unfold exactly as it was meant to.

Full Circle

In the months that followed, Arya's role in the community became one of quiet leadership, of being a guide and a mentor for those who were navigating their own paths of growth. She no longer felt the pressure to do everything herself—instead, she trusted the people around her to carry the work forward, knowing that each person brought their own unique gifts to the table.

One evening, as Arya stood by the river watching the sunset, she thought about how far she had come. From the girl who had once questioned her purpose and struggled to find her place, to the woman who had learned to trust herself and the flow of life, Arya realized that she had come full circle. Her journey had led her back to the place where it had all begun, but she was no longer the same person she had been before.

She had grown, she had learned, and she had healed. And now, as she looked out at the horizon, Arya knew that the journey would continue—always evolving, always expanding, always bringing new opportunities for growth and transformation.

But for now, Arya was content. She had found peace in the present moment, in the knowledge that life would continue to guide her, and in the deep understanding that her purpose wasn't something to be found—it was something to be lived.

As the sun dipped below the horizon, casting the sky in shades of gold and pink, Arya smiled, feeling the quiet joy of being exactly where she was meant to be.

And in that moment, Arya knew that the journey had only just begun.

Epilogue: The Eternal Journey

A Moment of Reflection

Years had passed since Arya first set out on the journey to find her purpose, and as she sat in her small, sunlit home, surrounded by the quiet beauty of nature, she marveled at how much her life had transformed. What had once been a restless search for meaning had blossomed into a deep, abiding sense of peace. Arya no longer felt the need to define her purpose in rigid terms or to measure her worth by external accomplishments. Instead, she had come to understand that her purpose was woven into the fabric of her everyday life, in the small moments of connection, love, and presence.

The lessons she had learned throughout her journey had become an intrinsic part of who she was. From her time in the village abroad, to her leadership in the community, to her deep spiritual exploration, Arya had come to realize that life was not about finding answers, but about embracing the questions. It was about being fully present in each moment, allowing herself to be guided by her heart, and trusting that the path would unfold exactly as it was meant to.

One morning, as Arya walked along the familiar riverbank, she paused to sit beneath the oak tree that had been her sanctuary since childhood. The river, with its steady, flowing current, had always reminded Arya of the journey of life—the way it carried her forward, sometimes gently, sometimes with force, but always in motion. And like the river, Arya's life had been a series of twists and turns, challenges and triumphs, each moment shaping her into the person she had become.

As she sat beneath the tree, listening to the soothing sound of the water, Arya closed her eyes and breathed deeply, feeling the warmth of the sun on her face. She was at peace—not because she had reached a final destination, but because she had learned to trust the process. She had learned that life was not about arriving, but about becoming.

The Gift of Presence

As Arya reflected on her journey, she thought about the people who had been part of her story—the guides, the mentors, the friends who had walked alongside her at different stages of her life. Each person had left an imprint on her heart, teaching her valuable lessons about love, compassion, resilience, and trust.

Leila, her childhood friend who had always been there to remind her of the importance of following her heart, remained a constant presence in Arya's life. Their friendship had deepened over the years, evolving from the carefree bond of youth into a relationship built on mutual respect and shared experiences. Whenever Arya felt uncertain or needed a sounding board for her thoughts, Leila was always there to listen, to offer her wisdom, and to remind Arya of her own strength.

Jaden, who had stepped into his role as the leader of the organization with such confidence and dedication, had become one of Arya's most trusted allies. Their paths had intertwined in ways neither of them had expected, and together, they had created a community rooted in kindness, support, and shared growth. Watching Jaden thrive in his leadership role had been one of the greatest joys of Arya's life, a reminder that true leadership was about empowering others to step into their own light.

But most of all, Arya thought about her family—her mother, whose quiet strength had always been a source of inspiration, and her sister, Rhea, whose journey into her own life had mirrored Arya's in so many ways. They had walked their paths together, each learning to embrace the changes that life brought, each supporting the other through moments of uncertainty and joy.

In these relationships, Arya had found the true gift of presence—the ability to be fully with someone, to listen with an open heart, and to offer love without expectation. It was this gift, more than anything else, that Arya had come to cherish in her life.

The Infinite Journey

As Arya sat by the river, she smiled to herself, knowing that her
journey was far from over. Life, she had learned, was a series of
cycles—beginnings and endings, growth and renewal, each phase
leading into the next in a beautiful, endless dance. The lessons she had
learned were not fixed; they would continue to evolve as she did,
guiding her through new experiences, new challenges, and new
opportunities for growth.

There would always be more to discover, more to explore, more to
learn. Arya no longer needed the certainty of a clearly defined path.
She had embraced the unknown, trusting that whatever came next
would be exactly what she needed.

And while Arya had spent so much of her life searching for answers,
she now understood that the journey was not about finding the
ultimate truth—it was about learning to live with the questions, to
embrace the mystery of existence, and to find joy in the unfolding of
each new day.

As she stood up from her place by the river and began to walk back
home, Arya felt a sense of lightness in her heart. She was no longer
searching—she was simply living. And in that living, she had found
the peace she had been seeking all along.

A Legacy of Love

In the years that followed, Arya continued to live her life with purpose, though her definition of purpose had shifted. She no longer felt the need to change the world in grand, sweeping ways. Instead, she focused on the small, meaningful moments that made up the fabric of her everyday life—the conversations with friends, the quiet acts of kindness, the moments of deep connection with the people around her.

Her work in the community continued to flourish, though Arya's role had become more of a quiet guide than a central figure. She was there to offer support, to mentor those who sought her wisdom, and to share the lessons she had learned along the way. But Arya no longer needed to be at the forefront—she was content to stand in the background, watching as the seeds she had planted continued to grow.

As the years passed, Arya's legacy became one not of accolades or accomplishments, but of love. She had touched countless lives, not through grand gestures, but through the simple act of being present, of offering compassion and understanding to those who crossed her path. And in the end, that was the legacy Arya had always wanted to leave behind—a legacy of love, of kindness, and of connection.

The Journey Continues

As Arya looked toward the future, she felt a deep sense of gratitude for the life she had lived. She had walked many paths, learned many lessons, and shared many moments of joy and sorrow with the people she loved. But more than anything, Arya was grateful for the journey itself—the journey that had taught her to trust herself, to trust the process, and to trust the unfolding of life.

And as she stood once again by the river, watching the water flow steadily toward the horizon, Arya smiled, knowing that the journey was far from over.

Because life, she had learned, was an eternal journey—one that would continue to lead her forward, guiding her toward new discoveries, new connections, and new opportunities for growth.

And in that knowing, Arya found the peace she had always been seeking.

Don't miss out!

Visit the website below and you can sign up to receive emails whenever AMEYA VATSA publishes a new book. There's no charge and no obligation.

https://books2read.com/r/B-A-BNMKC-MQAAF

Did you love *The Home Chosen*? Then you should read *Whispers from the Realms*[1] by AMEYA VATSA!

When the world begins to unravel, can one woman's awakening be the key to restoring balance?

Amara's life was ordinary—until the night the whispers began. Drawn into vivid dreams of a mysterious realm where light and darkness are intertwined, Amara's world starts to shift in ways she can't explain. As her connection to unseen forces deepens, she discovers she is part of something much bigger—a universal awakening that threatens to tear the fabric of reality apart.

---

1. https://books2read.com/u/mvpqX2

2. https://books2read.com/u/mvpqX2

Guided by spirit guides and haunted by shadows from within, Amara must face storms both inside herself and in the world around her. Along with a circle of fellow seekers, she uncovers the hidden truths of the universe—truths that challenge everything she thought she knew about life, death, and the nature of the soul.

But as the lines between the physical world and the spiritual realms blur, darker forces begin to emerge, resisting the awakening. Amara is thrust into a battle not just for her soul but for the fate of humanity. In a journey that takes her to the very edge of reality, she must confront her deepest fears, embrace both light and darkness and unlock the power hidden within her.

Whispers from the Realms is a spiritual guide in the form of a fantasy novel that weaves together mystery, adventure, and profound metaphysical insights.

For readers who crave a story of spiritual awakening, inner transformation, and the ultimate battle between light and darkness, this book will leave you questioning the very nature of existence—and your place in it.

The storm may rage, but within you is the calm. Within you is the light.

And that light can never be extinguished.

Also by AMEYA VATSA

Whispers from the Realms
The Home Chosen

About the Author

Ameya Vatsa, legally known as **Ankita Kumari**, is an author who explores themes of spiritual awakening, personal transformation, and the deeper mysteries of existence. Drawing from both personal experiences and spiritual insights, Ameya weaves intricate tales that resonate with readers seeking more than just entertainment—those who yearn for understanding and connection.

When not writing, Ankita enjoys reading, painting, and collecting real stories, continually finding inspiration in both the seen and unseen world.